T0106521

EYEWITNESS TO MURDER

I was still smiling when I pulled up my laptop and navigated to Pet Haven's website. I could hear the storm getting louder, and the Internet site that had been clear earlier in the day was staticky and slower tonight. I finally caught a glimpse of Aggie. She had moved from the bearskinned rug to the cot, which was littered with stuffed animals. I was just about to turn off the screen when it flickered and then jumped to a view of one of the other cameras. I clicked around the menu on several links, which switched from one room to another in search of the link that would take me back to Aggie. Just about to give up, I clicked on a link that showed a woman spraying down the outside area of the kennels. It appeared to be raining there, too, but, the kennel area was covered. I squinted to make out who the woman was. It looked like the owner, Keri Lynn Simpson. She wore a yellow rain slicker and boots. I was glad to see Pet Haven was true to their brochures and cleaned every night. Her back was to the camera. She must have gotten a call because she moved the hose to her left hand and pulled out her cell phone. She glanced at the phone and then returned it to her pocket.

I was just about to shut down when a shadow approached her from behind. That was when I saw a man's arm reach around and grab her from the back. He put his hands around her neck and squeezed.

She dropped the hose and clawed at the man's arms and face, but it was too little, too late.

She slid to the ground.

What did I just see? What just happened?

Thunder clapped, and my screen went black...

Books by V.M. Burns

Mystery Bookshop Series
THE PLOT IS MURDER
READ HERRING HUNT
THE NOVEL ART OF MURDER
WED, READ & DEAD

Dog Club Series
IN THE DOG HOUSE
THE PUPPY WHO KNEW TOO MUCH
BARK IF IT'S MURDER

Published by Kensington Publishing Corporation

Bark If It's Murder

V.M. Burns

LYRICAL UNDERGROUND
Kensington Publishing Corp.
www.kensingtonbooks.com

LYRICAL UNDERGROUND BOOKS are published by

Kensington Publishing Corp.
119 West 40th Street
New York, NY 10018

All Kensington titles, imprints, and distributed lines are available at special quantity discounts for bulk purchases for sales promotion, premiums, fund-raising, educational, or institutional use.

Special book excerpts or customized printings can also be created to fit specific needs. For details, write or phone the office of the Kensington Sales Manager: Kensington Publishing Corp., 119 West 40th Street, New York, NY 10018. Attn. Sales Department. Phone: 1-800-221-2647.

Lyrical Underground and Lyrical Underground logo Reg. US Pat. & TM Off.

First Electronic Edition: August 2019
eISBN-13: 978-1-5161-0789-6
eISBN-10: 1-5161-0789-6

First Print Edition: August 2019
ISBN-13: 978-1-5161-0792-6
ISBN-10: 1-5161-0792-6

Printed in the United States of America

Acknowledgments

As always, I want to thank Dawn Dowdle at Blue Ridge Literary Agency; and my editor, John Scognamiglio, and all of the great people at Kensington.

Thanks to Anthony "Trooper Tony" Cameron and to your TBI friends for answering my questions. Thanks to my work family (Chuck, Jill, Lindsey, and Tim), and to our leader, Sandy Morrison, for being so supportive (I hope I can return the favor one day). I'm grateful for my wonderful team (Amber, Derrick, Eric, Jennifer, Jonathan, and Robin). I truly appreciate the amazing Training Team who do so much to support me (Tena, Grace, Jamie, Deborah, and Kristie). Y'all are the best. Special thanks to Monica Jill, Linda Kay, and Weyman for being such good sports.

If it weren't for the wonderful memories I had as a member of Echo Dog Club in Buchanan, Michigan, this series would not have happened. So I want to thank all of my amazing Echo friends. Thank you to Eva Marie Mitchell (Dreem Poodles) for fact-checking my conformation details. Thanks to Becky Rae Halsey and Stephen Bryant for helping with the techie speak. Thanks to Debra Ramish, Deb Childs, and Dr. Jan Sanders for allowing me to pick your brains.

None of these books would be possible without the love and support of my family. Thank you, Benjamin Burns and Jackie Rucker; Jillian, Marcella and Drew Merkel; and Christopher, Carson, and Crosby Rucker.

I wouldn't be able to do any of this without my buddies Sophia Muckerson and Shelitha Mckee. Thank you both for listening and keeping me sane through all of the madness.

Chapter 1

"Is that a cow?"

Dixie snorted from the back seat. "Didn't you have cows in Indiana?"

I turned around in my seat and looked around the car seat's headrest. "We do have cows in Indiana in the country, but not in the city. Cows belong in the country. I'm a city girl."

Monica Jill pulled the car into the driveway and eagerly turned to face me. "It's just a few cows. They're behind a fence." She pointed to the fence across the road.

I shook my head. "Nope. No cows."

She sighed. "Cows weren't on your list."

The list my Realtor was referring to was my list of "must-haves" and "deal breakers" for my new home.

Monica Jill held up her hand and ticked items off. "No mountains or steep hills, no basement garages, no bears, coyotes, snakes, and now... cows." She sighed. "Three bedrooms, two baths, in your price point, which aren't on a mountain or hill or near any type of wildlife, is challenging, especially in Chattanooga."

"You can afford to raise your budget," Dixie said tentatively.

This was a conversation we'd had before. Technically, I could afford a much more expensive house than the limits I'd set for myself. I'd been frugal with the money from selling the house I'd shared with my husband in Indiana. I was determined not to touch the life insurance money, preferring to create trusts for our children. Stephanie and David were both grown and on their own. Stephanie was a lawyer in Chicago, and David was an actor in New York. I couldn't help but think at some point they would marry or purchase homes and I wanted to be able to help them. However, I didn't need to look back at Dixie to know she was alluding to the million dollars my husband had socked away in an offshore bank account before he was murdered. However, I wasn't comfortable touching that money, at least not until the police investigation was over.

"The housing market here is super hot and it's not easy finding properties that meet all of your criteria and now I need to eliminate all houses that are close to cows?" Monica Jill looked at me over her tortoiseshell and mother-of-pearl glasses. She was a thin woman with long, dark-brown hair and brown eyes.

"Yep. That's what I'm saying." I stared back at her.

The look on her face almost made me feel sorry for her. It had to be difficult for a Realtor to spend hours driving people like me around, burning up their gas, especially since she wouldn't get paid unless I bought a house. As of this minute, I estimated she'd shown me fifty-two houses. I'd never considered myself a difficult client, but apparently I was. Living in the foothills of the Appalachian Mountains meant finding a house that wasn't on a mountain or a steep hill was challenging. Few homes had all of my must-haves.

"I'm hungry. Let's eat and talk about our next move." She backed her car out of the driveway, all the time mumbling under her breath about cows.

Monica Jill drove to a seafood restaurant in downtown Chattanooga which was known for its shrimp and grits. I'd admit, prior to moving south, shrimp and grits was not a combination that would have appealed to me. In fact, grits wasn't exactly on my top-twenty list of favorite foods. However, the spicy dish had grown on me. While we ate and sipped sweet tea, another Southern favorite, we talked about options.

Monica Jill pulled up the Multiple Listing Service app on her phone and showed me the homes that fit her filter, and I acknowledged that pickings were slim. Monica Jill Nelson was a devout Christian with an almost sickeningly optimistic disposition. We met in the dog obedience class Dixie taught at the Eastern Tennessee Dog Club. Now we were both members of the Eastern Tennessee Dog Club and were enrolled for a second round of basic training. My toy poodle, Aggie, was an exceptionally smart dog, as was Monica Jill's dog, Jac, a mutt with lots of personality and a genuine zest for life. After a relatively short period of time with Dixie, we both realized our dogs needed a firm hand and consistent training. Jac was a rambunctious puppy who, according to Dixie, needed a way to release energy to stay out of trouble. At three, Aggie was older and more devious. Her training was more to teach me than her. After a few weeks in class, I realized Monica Jill was a Realtor and enlisted her help to find a forever home for Aggie and me.

Monica Jill swiped her phone with one hand and shoveled food into her mouth with the other. "If you aren't willing to raise your budget or reduce your *deal breaker* list, are you willing to consider a house that needs a bit of updating?"

I thought about it for a minute. "Maybe. It depends on how much work."

She smiled. "Great. When we finish eating, we'll go take a look at another house." She picked up her phone and dialed a number.

"Wait, where is it?"

Before she could answer me, the scheduling office picked up and she arranged a showing.

Dixie and I exchanged a glance.

Dixie raised a finely arched brow and stared at Monica Jill, then shrugged and continued eating. Dixie and I had been friends in college, but we'd lost touch. After graduation, she'd moved back to Chattanooga and married her high school sweetheart, Beauregard "Beau" Jefferson. I married Albert, and after the children, Dixie and I drifted apart. A few months ago, Albert decided to trade me in like one of the cars on his used car lot for a woman named Bambi who was younger than our children. That was when I decided to make some much-needed life changes. I decided to move someplace warm and sunny and reconnected with my old friend.

Scarlett "Dixie" Jefferson was a big woman. At close to six feet, Dixie was a Southern belle with big Dolly Parton hair and a bigger personality to match, and a heart as big as the Tennessee River.

After lunch, Monica Jill drove us to what she called a "transitional neighborhood" near the last house I'd rented. Due to a series of unfortunate events, which involved a dead body and the police believing I'd murdered my landlord, I had moved out and was back in a hotel with my dog and desperate to find permanent housing.

The neighborhood was off of a major street, but unlike most of the properties I'd seen so far, this one wasn't in a subdivision or the country. I liked it. Not just because there was no association fee, but I liked the fact this was an actual neighborhood with an eclectic mixture of houses, unlike the area where I moved from in Indiana where all the houses were basically the same except with different color siding. I also liked that there was no group with the power to dictate everything from the number of pets I could have to whether or not I had a fence. Even the rental had a neighborhood association that controlled the length of the grass and the types of Christmas decorations allowed. In all fairness, most of the association's rules were fair and reasonable, but I had spent too many years listening to others—from my late husband to a neighborhood group—to allow myself to continue to be ruled by anyone else. I was now determined to find my happy place and enjoy my life once and for all.

The house we stopped at was a single-story house built in the 1980s. The inside reflected the best and the worst of the decade. From the amazing wall of windows that overlooked the backyard to the vaulted ceilings in the great room to the mauve floral wallpaper and coordinating border.

"Why did anyone think a black sunken tub was a good idea?" Dixie stared at the master bath and shook her head.

I quietly roamed from room to room.

"This carpet is unfortunate." Monica Jill frowned at the striped carpeting that had undoubtedly been picked to coordinate with the wallpaper. "Maybe there are hardwoods underneath." She perked up and walked to the corner of the room and tried to pry an edge away from the vent. After a bit of work, she dropped the carpet and replaced the vent. "Bummer."

I opened one of the three sliding glass doors that overlooked the backyard. I stepped outside onto a faded, threadbare well-worn green carpet.

The yard was large and completely fenced in by an old wooden privacy fence that was weathered and obviously had seen better days. There were gaps where boards had come off and been filled in with hog wire to prevent anything larger than a small squirrel from escaping. The grass and plantings were overgrown, and a large koi pond sat covered by leaves. Stale, stagnant water, which had accumulated over the years, sent up a pungent aroma that caused even the ever-optimistic Monica Jill to frown.

I shocked the frown off her face by saying, "I like it."

Both Monica Jill and Dixie turned to stare at me as though I'd suddenly lost my mind.

"Are you serious?" Dixie asked.

"It needs work, but—"

"That's an understatement." She laughed.

I stared at the house. "It has good potential." I spent the next twenty minutes explaining what needed to be done and what this house could become.

Both Dixie and Monica Jill were shocked, but both recognized the house had "good bones." Years of watching design shows on HGTV had made me a believer of what a house could become with a little work, and by the end, they were both not only enthusiastic, but supportive. We walked out after nearly an hour in the house with a plan for a renovation that would turn this 1980s remodel into a contemporary gem.

Monica Jill locked up while Dixie and I explored the neighborhood. When we'd arrived, I hadn't noticed that the house next door was also for sale. We took a few minutes to check it out too.

Similar to its neighbor, this house was also built in the eighties. However, a quick glance in the front window showed this contemporary home to have been renovated inside.

When Monica Jill joined us, we asked to see the inside.

"This house isn't showing up in the MLS." She swiped her cell phone and quickly dialed the listing agent whose name was on the sign. While she talked, Dixie and I walked around back. Just like the house next door, this house had a huge fenced-in backyard. However, instead of a koi pond and overgrown landscaping, this home had a massive deck that went around the side of the house and extended well out into the yard. The deck had been built around several mature trees and bore the outline of a pool, which was now gone.

"Wow." Dixie whistled.

Crepe myrtle, dogwood, Bradford pear, and crab apple trees, along with several I couldn't identify, provided a canopy of shade that would be beautiful when in bloom and a nightmare in the fall when the leaves fell.

The listing agent gave Monica Jill the okay to show us the property and the code to unlock the key box on the back door.

The house wasn't large, but unlike its neighbor, this one had undergone renovations at some point during the past few decades. Instead of the hideous striped carpet that existed next door, this house had hardwood floors in the public areas. All wallpaper had been removed, and the walls were painted a neutral gray. The three bedrooms were carpeted, and the master bedroom and bath had recently had the glass block that was still in place next door, removed. This house wasn't new construction perfect, but it was livable. While talking to Dixie and Monica Jill about the remodeling needed next door, I had gotten excited about the idea of a project and putting my own stamp on my house. Walking through this house helped me put into perspective the total amount of work needed.

"So, what do you think?" Dixie asked tentatively.

I gazed out onto the deck. "I think I want to place an offer."

Monica Jill smiled. "Great. Which house?"

"This one."

Dixie let out a breath. "Thank God."

I smiled. "I thought you liked the house next door?"

She nodded. "I do like the house. I like both houses, but the other one needs a *lot* more work. At least, if you want to make renovations to this house, you can still live in it."

"Agreed."

Monica Jill smiled. "Well, that's great. My office is just around the corner. Let's hightail it over there and get our offer in. According to Matt, the listing agent, he's expecting another offer and we want to get ours in as soon as possible."

She drove us the short distance to her office, and I waited while she pulled up a mountain of papers for me to sign.

"I'm going home. I've still got a lot to do before the show tomorrow." Dixie stared at Monica Jill and me. "Don't forget, you both signed up to work the dog show."

We both nodded.

In addition to teaching canine obedience classes at the Eastern Tennessee Dog Club (ETDC), Dixie's dogs had competed in various dog sports, including conformation and obedience. Now that her two standard poodles, Champion Chyna 9th Wonder of the World and Grand Champion Galactic Imperial Resistance Leader, or "Chyna" and "Leia" for short, were retired from competition, Dixie had become a judge. She was judging poodles at a large dog show, and the ETDC had signed on to work the show. Monica Jill and I, along with the other members of Dixie's dog class, had eagerly volunteered to help. Despite Dixie's warnings that it wouldn't be anything like the glamour we saw on television from the Westminster Kennel Club, we were all excited.

It took a lot longer to complete the myriad of paperwork needed to put an offer on a house than I thought it would. It was certainly a lot more than I remembered from when Albert and I bought our house, but then a lot had changed in the nearly quarter century. Eventually, everything was signed, dated, initialed, and submitted. I left Monica Jill at her office and drove the short distance to my hotel to anxiously await the owners' response and question whether or not I should have offered more, knowing I was most likely entering a potential multiple bid situation. I questioned if I should have gone in with a higher bid to entice the sellers to ignore other offers or if I should have followed Monica Jill's suggestion to leave room for negotiation. Should I have bit the bullet and not asked the sellers to pay my closing costs as Dixie had suggested and just shelled out the extra cash? I tried to ease my mind and push these thoughts away, but nothing worked. So I hoped a walk would provide a much-needed distraction from thoughts of the house and would tire out both me and my six-pound dog, Aggie, to the point that we would both sleep soundly.

I grabbed Aggie's leash and we headed outside. Chattanooga in mid-January was still sunny, but there was a chill in the air today, which made me walk faster than usual and made me impatient about lingering while Aggie sniffed every blade of grass and tracked scent trails for every creature to have crossed this path. I tugged on her leash and ignored the look in her eyes that begged to be allowed to explore a dead bird carcass.

Our extended-stay hotel was located near the interstate, which made my commute to work easy but kept me awake late into the night, listening to the sounds of cars and semis flying along Interstate 75. Options for hotels that allowed pets were limited, so the traffic noise was a trade-off for a clean room that accepted pets without requiring a nonrefundable pet fee that was the equivalent to the going rate for an organ on the black market. At least, that was what my friend Red told me. A few weeks of dating a Tennessee Bureau of Investigations Officer had provided all kinds of miscellaneous facts that would scare most people.

I walked to a nearby field, which was far enough away from the interstate and traffic that I didn't have to worry about Aggie's safety, and I took her off-leash, making sure I had the dried liver in my pocket. The pungent-smelling treat had proven over weeks of obedience classes to be the one thing that would entice her to come running whenever the small container was opened.

Leash removed and nothing but a wide-open space in front of her lit a fuse in the little black dog's soul. She ran with a reckless abandon and zeal that brought a smile to my face as I watched her run in circles for the sheer joy of running. I thought of the large fenced-in yard at the house and knew I had made the right choice. Despite the cold weather, I let Aggie run until I noticed her slow down.

"Aggie, come."

She stopped and turned to look in my direction.

I took the leash out of my pocket and waited. She took one step in my direction and then lifted her nose in the air and sniffed. Even from the distance that separated us, I could tell she had gotten a whiff of something, and the look in her eyes told me it wasn't the dried liver treats.

I fumbled to remove the plastic container but wasn't quick enough. Before I could get the lid off, Aggie took off in the opposite direction with a gleam in her eyes that told me she was up to no good.

Despite the weeks of training I'd endured, during which Dixie drilled into me the importance of not repeating commands, I ran toward my dog screaming, "Aggie, come."

Aggie stopped only when she found the odor she'd detected. I was feet away when I realized what she'd smelled.

"Aggie, NO!"

I felt like I was watching a movie in slow motion as I ran toward her. By now, Aggie was on her back and rolling with what appeared to be a smile on her face.

Panting with her tongue extended, she rushed to me and pounced on my legs. She reeked of deer poop.

"Ewww." I turned away and tried to block my nose. Despite my best efforts, the aroma infiltrated my nasal passages. I looked at my beautiful dog, happy as could be with grass and the remains of her romp through the field attached to her backside.

I stared at her face, which radiated with joy, and wondered how we were going to make it back to the hotel. It was too late to take her to the groomers. I checked my coat pockets and couldn't find anything more than a few receipts to help remove the excess solids. I sighed, took a deep breath, and attached her leash. Then I used my last two gas receipts to remove the clumps of fecal matter from her coat. One whiff told me the receipts had been ineffective.

I sighed and made the walk of shame back to the hotel while frantically trying to remember where I'd left my rubber gloves and whether or not I still had dog shampoo. If I wanted a distraction to get my mind off the house, Aggie had certainly provided it.

Chapter 2

The next day I awoke early when the alarm on my cell phone went off at four. It was still dark outside and while I had set the alarm, I still cursed the idea of having to get up so early. I stood up and stretched. Even Aggie thought I'd lost my mind and curled up in a tight ball in the warm area I vacated in the bed rather than getting up. I stuck my tongue out at her. I shuffled to the shower.

The warm water from the shower pelted my skin and revived my mind to the possibilities of the day. After I showered, I hurried to my phone to check for messages from Monica Jill. She'd warned me not to be disappointed if I didn't hear from her until later, but I was disappointed anyway when there was no message. I tried to push thoughts of the house out of my mind and rummaged through the closet to find something appropriate to wear to the dog show.

Visions of the Westminster Dog Show flashed through my mind, of men in suits and women in dresses and comfortable shoes trotting around the rings. Dixie's instructions were to dress in comfortable clothes. Dog shows, she'd said, were dirty places unless you were sitting in the audience or competing. I put on a faded pair of jeans and a T-shirt and flipped on the television to listen to the news while I brushed my teeth. I was only half-listening when one of the roving reporters mentioned the dog show. I slipped out of the bathroom and turned up the volume. The reporter was pointing out all of the various events to be judged this weekend and encouraged viewers to come out. I glanced at my outfit and quickly changed into a pair of slacks and a nice blouse. This show might not be Westminster, but if there were going to be reporters, that meant it would be broadcast locally. I pulled my hair down from the ponytail and fired up my curling iron while I applied makeup.

Changing clothes meant I was running late and Aggie's morning walk was shorter than either of us would have liked. I'd been encouraged to arrive early, and each moment I delayed added to my anxiety. When I finally left for the dog show, I was forty-five minutes later than I'd originally planned.

I hopped onto the interstate and headed for the fairgrounds. It was still early, so the rush hour traffic wasn't bad, and I made it well ahead of the start of the festivities. However, the parking lot was filling up with RVs, campers, and cars, and I had quite a hike to get to the main building.

By the time I entered the arena, I was out of breath and panting. Perhaps I should have kept on the tennis shoes I'd originally planned rather than switching at the last minute to casual wedge heels.

I craned my neck and looked around until I spotted a familiar face and a bald head and headed for them.

Monica Jill stood sipping a coffee and eating a donut. She smiled and handed me a cup from a table. "There you are. We were afraid you'd overslept."

I took a sip from the steaming hot coffee and shook my head.

She looked me up and down with a raised eyebrow.

I noticed that while she wore makeup, her hair was pulled back into a ponytail and she was wearing a pair of old blue jeans, a T-shirt, and tennis shoes.

"What?"

She smiled. "Nothing. You look really nice."

The compliment sounded more like an accusation, but I chose to ignore it and turned to the bald head I'd recognized. "Hi, Dr. Morgan."

Dr. Morgan was short and bald, with an egg-shaped head that always reminded me of Mr. Potato Head. He was also in our dog obedience class with his German shepherd, Max, who was a vicious-looking pussycat with a giant crush on Aggie. He looked gruff and unshaven. He inclined his head, grunted, and sipped his coffee. He wore a faded Tennessee Vols T-shirt and jeans.

I was starting to think perhaps I'd dressed wrong when I saw Dixie in a suit along with the current ETDC president, a white-haired Amazon of a woman named Lenora Houston, but everyone called her "Lenny."

"Good morning, troops." Lenny took a wide-legged stance in front of us. She had a baseball cap pushed down and turned around backward over her short-cropped hair. She had on shorts and a T-shirt and wore a whistle around her neck like a military drill sergeant. "Gather 'round."

Considering there were so few of us, we were all pretty well gathered, but we each took a step forward and got closer to her.

Just as she started to speak, we heard footsteps rushing toward us. "Hold up. I'm coming." The last member of Dixie's obedience class, Bobbie Jean Thompson, B.J. to her friends, rushed to join us. The slightly plump African American woman had skin like dark chocolate and hair which she wore in long braids that trailed down her back. Today she had the braids pulled back into a ponytail that bobbed as she ran.

"I'm sorry I'm late." She leaned over and took several breaths. "Snowball wouldn't go potty and I—"

"Yes. Yes. We get the picture." Lenny lifted a page on her flip chart and pulled a pen from behind her ear. "Now, we have a busy day ahead and a lot of work to do."

Dixie took a step forward. "May I just say how grateful we are that you all *volunteered* to help out at the show. We know how busy everyone is and there are probably a hundred other things you could do, but we're so thankful you decided to help the club." She smiled and then glanced expectantly at Lenny.

"Yes. Yes." Lenny rocked on the balls of her feet and rolled her eyes.

Dixie sighed. "I have to go, but I know you all will be fine." She smiled and then walked away.

"Now that the niceties are over, let's get down to business." Lenny shoved her pen back behind her ear. "Follow me." She turned and marched off without a backward glance.

We hesitated for a split second and then hurried to catch up to her.

Monica Jill was thin and was in great shape, and she and Dr. Morgan took the lead. My casual shoes weren't intended for hiking, and as the sweat dripped down my armpits, I realized they weren't the best choice I could have made today.

B.J. huffed alongside me at the rear. "That woman is worse than a drill sergeant."

The fairgrounds were large and included a large stadium. We'd walked halfway around the arena before Lenny led us into a back storage room. By the time B.J. and I arrived, Lenny was standing, arms folded, inside the storage room, rocking.

B.J. leaned against the wall and caught her breath.

I was breathing heavily but felt a small sliver of joy when I noticed a bead of sweat fall from Dr. Morgan's nose.

"This is the main storage closet and the location where you will get your supplies."

I looked around. "Supplies?"

Lenny reached up on a shelf and pulled down a large box labeled PAPER TOWELS. She ripped the box open and pulled out a large roll. She handed one to each of us.

"What's this for?" I asked.

"Cleanup." She turned and pulled spray bottles of ammonia off another shelf and handed one to each of us.

"Cleanup?" I stared from the paper towel roll to the ammonia. It took several moments before all of my mental cylinders engaged. Once the reality of what she was saying set in, I was horrified. "You have got to be joking!"

Lenny had just turned around with pooper-scoopers in each hand. She stood ramrod-straight and looked at me as though I was insane. "I don't joke."

"You mean we have to clean up poop?" Monica Jill asked.

Lenny nodded. "That's exactly what I mean."

"But…it's a dog show?" I tried to focus. "There are going to be hundreds of dogs."

She nodded. "Exactly, that's why you're needed." She shook her head. "If it wasn't for the pooper cleanup crew, there'd be dog crap a mile long. No one would be able to take a step without stepping in it."

B.J. clutched her roll of paper towels and said in a small voice, "But Miss Dixie told us responsible pet owners clean up after their dogs."

"True. However, at a dog show, no one has time for that." She must have noticed the forlorn look in everyone's eyes. "Well, some handlers will clean up after their dogs, but most won't."

"So we're supposed to walk around and clean up…poop?" Monica Jill asked.

Lenny nodded. "Not just walk around." She handed us garbage bags. "If a dog has an accident in one of the rings, then you'll need to go and clean it up. They'll announce it over the loudspeaker, and one of you, whoever's closest, will hurry into the ring and clean it up."

"But, that's going to be …horrible. We'll be filthy." I looked at my slacks and not-at-all-comfortable shoes.

"Not really dressed to work a dog show. You should have worn clothes you didn't care about." She frowned.

"Surely there has to be a better way of dealing with this…ah…problem." Dr. Morgan scowled.

Lenny folded her arms across her chest and rocked. "Look, this show is important for ETDC. They're paying us a thousand dollars per day to clean up poop." She looked from one of us to the other. "Three days of work for that amount of money will pay our mortgage for the next three months."

We stood in silence.

"We all have to do our part." She rocked on the balls of her feet.

After a few seconds, each of us nodded.

"Good. Now, get out there and make ETDC proud."

The next few hours were a hideously smelly, disgusting nightmare. We ran from one end of the arena to the other. Every few minutes, there was an announcement that sent one of us running. "CLEANUP IN RING…" The announcer filled in the number of the ring or the breed being judged.

At the start of the show, things were slow, and I was able to note that in addition to hundreds of dogs competing, there were vendors selling dog paraphernalia for every breed and every interest. Everything from breed-inspired jewelry to special dog beds, cages, leashes, and clothing. The clothing in particular caught my attention and I quickly bought a T-shirt, shorts, socks, and tennis shoes covered in poodles. I made a quick change in the restroom and contemplated dumping my discarded clothes in the nearest garbage receptacle. However, a quick glance at the label in the back of the shirt reminded me the blouse had been a gift from my daughter, Stephanie, and had probably cost a small fortune. Instead, I dumped the clothes into a shopping bag and left them in a locker in the storage room where Lenny had instructed us to leave any valuables.

Cleaning up dog poop had to be the worst job ever. It wasn't just the thought of scooping poop. I got over that pretty quickly. No, it was more than just the fecal matter. It was the stooping down and spraying of ammonia and then scrubbing with a paper towel to prevent other dogs from smelling the area and then relieving themselves in the same spot. I learned my lesson when I was called to clean up after a borzoi in the hound group. I learned from the announcer that borzois were Russian sighthounds. After cleaning up what turned out to be a large amount of poop, I hurried out of the ring, only to be called back when a Sicilian coursing hound I'd never heard of before, a Cirneco dell'Etna, promptly squatted and relieved herself in the exact same spot I'd just cleaned. Unfortunately for me, Lenny was nearby and marched me into the ring to oversee my cleaning endeavors. When the area was cleaner than the table where I'd eaten a snack earlier, she escorted me out of the ring and reprimanded me in front of everyone.

By lunchtime, my knees, back, and neck ached. My nose burned from sniffing so much ammonia and my head throbbed. I flopped down at a picnic table where the vendors were set up and tried to get the aroma of ammonia and the thought of how I'd just spent the last four hours of my day out of my head—at least enough to contemplate eating. I tried to remind myself this was going to generate a lot of money for the dog club. Besides, it was just one day. I tried to shake off my mood.

B.J. flopped down across from me. "I'm wore out." She sighed. "I don't want to see another piece of sh—"

"CLEANUP IN THE TERRIER GROUP."

She let out a long breath and hoisted herself up. "That's me." She hurried off.

I waved and looked around. Nearby was a display booth with a sign advertising a high-end doggie day care.

"Lilly!"

I jumped as Monica Jill waved her hand in front of my face. "You scared me to death."

She smiled. "You were miles away. I've called you three times."

"Sorry."

She smiled. "Guess what?"

At that moment, my brain wasn't firing on all cylinders. "Lenny wants me to clean up after elephants coming to the circus?"

She laughed. "No, but I wouldn't put it past her." She smiled expectantly. When I didn't respond, she put her hand on her hip and stomped a foot. "I can't believe you can't guess."

I shook my head. "Sorry, I think all of the ammonia has damaged my brain cells." I held up my spray bottle.

She sighed. "The owners accepted your offer. You just bought a house!"

Even after she spelled it out, it took a few moments for my brain to remember what she was talking about. When the reality sank in, I leapt up and gave her a hug. "Thank you!"

"You're welcome!"

We talked about the next steps, which involved getting an inspection and sending the signed sales contract to my bank to start the mortgage process.

"Now, what had you so engrossed that I nearly had to slap you to get your attention?"

I pointed to the booth for Pet Haven.

"They're fantastic. I take Jac there two days per week."

I cocked my head to the side to stare at her better. "Are you serious? Doggie day care? What is it?"

"Oh, honey, you need to take Aggie. She'd love it. You drop your dog off in the morning and they get to play and run and get rid of some of their pent-up energy. Aggie's small so she might not be as wild and crazy as Jac, but it was either day care or I was going to have to take him back to the shelter." She shook her head. "Dixie recommended I look into it."

"Aggie isn't as rambunctious as Jac, but she's smart and Dixie said she gets bored when I'm at work. So, she gets into trouble." I looked over at the sign again. "I wonder if it would be a good idea for her."

Monica Jill linked arms with me. "Let's go over and find out." She guided me over to the booth.

Pet Haven Pet Resort and Doggie Day Care had a booth that was much more elaborate than the pop-up tents and umbrellas over tables that most of the other vendors brought. Their tent was a four-sided one that had round-topped windows on two of the sides. One side was unzipped and folded back to reveal a spacious interior. It looked as though hardwood floors covered the ground and a crystal chandelier dangled from the center of the tent. Inside the tent was furnished with comfortable furniture and a large television.

"Wow!" I stared at the inside thinking how much nicer this tent looked than my hotel room.

A man and a woman were engaged in an embrace but immediately separated.

"Welcome!" A tall, thin, beautiful woman with flawless skin, who looked like a supermodel, walked forward and extended her hand.

I wiped my hand on my T-shirt before shaking. Something about her perfectly arched brows and neatly coiffed hair in this immaculate upscale tent made me feel small and dirty.

The man gave one glance at the woman before sidling past us and making his exit from the tent.

Monica Jill didn't seem to feel any discomfort. She smiled broadly, then walked up and gave the woman a hug. "Keri Lynn, I thought I recognized you." The two women embraced. "You're looking as beautiful as ever."

Keri Lynn smiled. "Monica Jill, I didn't know you were involved with dog shows." She looked around. "Did you bring Jac?"

"Good Lord. No! Jac would be kicked out of here fast and in a hurry." She turned to me. "This is my good friend, Lilly Ann Echosby." She turned back to Keri Lynn. "This is Keri Lynn Simpson, owner of Pet Haven Pet Resort and Doggie Day Care."

We nodded an acknowledgment.

"Keri Lynn, you're just going to have to excuse us. We look a hot mess, but we're both members of the Eastern Tennessee Dog Club and we volunteered to help out today." She leaned close and whispered, "We've gotten stuck cleaning dog poop all day."

Keri Lynn smiled. "No worries. Some days I feel like that's all we do at Pet Haven."

The two friends chatted for a few minutes and I wandered around the tent and looked at the homey décor. I picked up the brochures that detailed their menu of services, which included day care, pet grooming, and boarding. Apparently, Pet Haven was a high-end, full-service facility.

"What kind of dog do you have?" Keri Lynn stood by my shoulder.

"I have a toy poodle named Aggie."

"Aggie is the cutest little thing." Monica Jill scrunched her shoulders and grinned. "I just want to pick her up and love on her every time I see her."

"She's cute, but she has her moments," I said. "Our obedience instructor, Dixie Jefferson, said she's smart and needs something to do."

Keri Lynn nodded. "Smart dogs without a job can get into a lot of trouble. Are you considering doggie day care?"

I nodded.

"I hope you'll consider Pet Haven. We have a wonderful day care program. There will be plenty of dogs for her to play with during the day, plus we have excellent security."

"Jac loves day care. As soon as we get to Pet Haven, he practically drags me inside. When he sees his buddies, he gets so excited and his little butt just wags." Monica Jill smiled and demonstrated the wag by wagging her body. "He loves to run and play. By the time he gets home, he's worn out." She smiled. "They have excellent staff who will toss his ball for hours."

"I've been reluctant to take Aggie because I worry about her getting hurt. She's such a little dog." I looked at Keri Lynn. "She only weighs six pounds."

"No need to worry. We have a separate play area for the little dogs and another one for puppies. She won't be playing with dogs that weigh more than twenty pounds. We're extremely careful about things like that."

Keri Lynn Simpson talked about all of the features of Pet Haven for several minutes, from the trained staff to the twenty-four-hour security and pet cams that allowed concerned pet parents to go online and watch their "fur babies" whenever they wanted. She also handed me a brochure that touted the benefits of boarding with Pet Haven. "At Pet Haven, your fur baby is a guest. Your dog isn't put in a cage all day and all night and only taken outside a few times a day, like at other boarding facilities. Our pet guests have their own rooms." She picked up a remote and pushed several buttons until pictures of the luxury accommodations popped up. The villas were actual rooms that included flat-screen televisions, aromatherapy, luxury bedding, private air-conditioned interior spaces, and a doggie door to their own private exterior space.

"Aromatherapy?" I looked at the brochure.

"Yes, that's standard for all of our guests. Although you will be pleased to know we have a wide variety of à la carte services that include everything from shiatsu massage to acupuncture for some of our older guests."

It took several seconds before I realized my mouth was open. I closed it and swallowed. "How much does something like that cost?"

I could tell by the way her lips pursed she found the discussion of cost distasteful. However, after a few seconds, she rattled off some figures that made my jaw drop again. She sniffed and shrugged. "We service a select clientele. Our patrons want only the best for their canine companions." She lifted her right hand and looked at her wrist, which held an expensive diamond Rolex.

She took a gold pen and scribbled something on the back of a business card with her left hand and then handed it to me. Keri Lynn smiled, but the smile never reached her eyes. I had been mentally dismissed.

The speaker announced cleanup was needed, and Monica Jill and I made our apologies and hurried back to work. I put the brochures in my pocket and promptly forgot about Pet Haven as I returned to my self-inflicted purgatory.

By the end of the day, every part of my body ached and an odor followed me to the point that I could only conclude the hideous odor was attached to some part of my being. In the parking lot, I removed my shoes and placed a garbage bag I'd stuffed in my pocket on the seat before getting in the car.

I drove back to the hotel and sat behind the wheel of the car for a full minute before I could muster up the strength to force my body to get out of the car. However, Aggie needed to be walked and fed. So, I forced my mind not to think about the pain as I got out and made my way in my socks from the parking lot to the room.

I put on a pair of slippers and quickly took Aggie outside so she could take care of business. It took longer than normal because Aggie was fascinated with all of the smells on my clothing and spent a long time sniffing my legs. Eventually, she gave me a break and did her business. After an entire day of cleaning up after dogs, it took every bit of willpower to force my body to bend over and clean up after my own dog. However, as B.J. had commented earlier, I still heard Dixie's voice in my head. *Responsible dog owners clean up after their pets.*

Back in the room, I ordered a pizza while I fed Aggie. When the pizza was delivered, I took it into the bathroom, peeled off my clothes, and sank into a hot bubble bath. The desk chair served as my table, and I took a bottle of wine from my small refrigerator and drank directly from the bottle while I soaked. Aggie scratched at the door and whined for admittance, but I knew from experience that my makeshift table wasn't tall enough to prevent a determined poodle from stealing a slice of pizza, and the hotel bed was too low for me to slide under to retrieve her.

I stayed in the tub so long my skin started to pucker, and I had to refresh the water three times. When I finally got out, I was stiff but felt clean, a feeling I had wondered if I would ever experience again. I entered the bedroom, where Aggie had nestled into the middle of the bed and was sound asleep. I quietly dressed for bed and completed the remainder of my nightly routine by walking to the door and double-checking the locks. The extended-stay hotel rooms, while not huge by any standard, were much larger than a traditional hotel room, which was one of the reasons I chose it. When I turned to face the bed, I realized Aggie had expressed her dissatisfaction for being excluded from pizza by ripping up a pillow. There was a mass of foam along with a personal deposit that would have rivaled the one left by the borzoi. The smell of the pizza along with my bubble bath had delayed the odor, but now that I'd seen it, it overpowered every other smell. For a split second, I contemplated poodlecide.

When I woke up on Saturday morning, I was stiff but not nearly as sore as the previous day. Aggie was snuggled next to me, sharing the one pillow she hadn't destroyed the previous night. When I opened my eyes, she immediately opened hers and her big brown eyes stared into mine. I wanted to be angry at her for the destruction she'd done the previous night. However, Dixie's words rang through my head. *Never discipline a dog if you did not see the offense happen.* I had nothing but the highest respect for my friend, but I wasn't so sure she was right that Aggie wouldn't understand why she was being disciplined if it wasn't done in the moment of the offense. I was sure I saw guilt staring out of her little face, plus something else. If I had to guess, I'd say it was a smirk of satisfaction.

Aggie yawned, and I got a whiff of doggie breath that reminded me I needed to make an appointment with my vet for a dental cleaning.

I stretched and got dressed. Today, I was thankful I hadn't volunteered to work the entire weekend. I wanted to see the dogs and support Dixie. My plan was to go as a spectator today, although the idea of returning caused me to groan out loud.

As I was leaving, my phone rang. I looked down and recognized my boss's name. "Hello, Linda Kay."

"Lilly, I'm so sorry to bother you on your weekend."

"It's no bother, but aren't you and Jacob supposed to be on your way to Atlanta for the art auction?"

"We don't leave until tomorrow, but I just got a call from Jacob. He went hiking on Lookout Mountain and fell."

"Oh. My. God. I hope he'll be okay."

"He's got a broken ankle. He'll be able to come back to work in a week, but he's in no shape to travel to Atlanta with me. So that's why I'm calling. I wondered if you would like to go?"

"Really?" I tried to hide my excitement, but I didn't think I did a good job.

She chuckled. "Yes, really. Now, you certainly don't have to go if you don't want to. There's no obligation."

I looked at my face in the mirror over the bureau and realized there was no way I could hide my elation and didn't even try. I screamed. "I'm sorry. I would love to go, but are you sure it's okay? I'm just a temporary employee, and I wouldn't want you to get in trouble with the board."

I could tell from her voice she was smiling. "I already talked to the board chairman and got his approval. So if you want to come, you're welcome."

"I'd love to come."

We finalized the details, and I was grinning when I hung up.

Linda Kay Weyman was the executive director for the Chattanooga Museum of Art, which was funded through the Hopewell Family Trust. Linda Kay and her assistant, Jacob Flemings, were full-fledged employees. I was a temp who was hired to straighten out the accounting mess left by the last Hopewell legacy, whom the trust was forced to hire. He hadn't had the slightest clue about accounting and the books were in bad shape. I'd spent most of my time getting things straightened out with the IRS and making sure the museum's nonprofit status was renewed. In the short time I'd worked at the museum, I was learning a lot about art. Linda Kay was an excellent teacher and a real classy lady.

She and Jacob had talked about the art auction a lot, and I had tried not to show my disappointment I wasn't going to have an opportunity to attend. Now things had changed, and I was going to a real art auction. I did a happy dance, which must have had Aggie concerned I was having a seizure, if the tilt of her head and the look on her face were any indication.

I scooped up my dog and we danced—well, I turned around in circles and Aggie clutched my sweater as though her life depended on it. When I finally settled down, the realization dawned on me that in order for me to attend the art auction in Atlanta, I'd need to make arrangements for Aggie. I could ask Dixie. She and her husband, Beau, loved poodles, and I knew they would spoil her as much as they had their own two standard poodles. That was when I remembered Dixie and Beau would be leaving on Monday for their anniversary trip to the mountains in Gatlinburg. They weren't even taking their own dogs with them. One of Beau's nephews was going to be keeping their dogs. I racked my brain. Maybe Red, my *gentleman friend*, would be able to stay, but Red was away at a special training camp for the Tennessee Bureau of Investigators. He'd be back on Monday night, but that was too late. I needed someone tomorrow. I stared into Aggie's expressive face and gave her a quick squeeze. I'd only been in Chattanooga a short time and hadn't made a lot of friends I would trust to take care of her yet. The realization that I would have to board her left me cold. I knew people boarded their dogs all the time. I wished my daughter, Stephanie, lived closer. Or even my son, David. I took a deep breath and released it slowly. "Maybe Pet Haven?" I remembered the card Keri Lynn had given me earlier. I scrambled to find where I'd shoved it and took a look. Keri Lynn had apparently felt the prices were too steep for me, which they were, but the card gave me a 20 percent discount on my first boarding stay. I looked at Aggie.

She gave my nose a lick, which brought a smile to my face.

"This is crazy. I'm worrying for no good reason," I reassured Aggie. "Pet Haven is an exclusive resort and spa. You'll be able to play and watch television. Maybe I'll even spring for the shiatsu massage treatment." I squeezed her and made a mental note to find out if Pet Haven accepted credit cards.

I fed Aggie and then took her outside to take care of business. I turned on the television to keep her company, one thing Pet Haven and I had in common. I briefly wondered what channel she would watch and then hurried out to the dog show.

Attending the dog show as a spectator was vastly different from attending as a professional pooper-scooper. I meandered around the grounds and admired the various breeds of dogs I'd barely glanced at the previous day. Many breeds I recognized, but far too many were dogs I'd never seen before, which I found fascinating. There were a lot of campers and RVs set up outside. Dogs were being bathed and groomed from one end of the grounds to the other. Few people walked without a brush in their hand and a small bait bag wrapped around their waists. As I learned from Dixie, bait bags were basically a small variation of a fanny pack used by dog trainers and competitors. They held treats used to "bait" or entice dogs.

I spent most of my time admiring the poodles, not just because I owned one but because I knew Dixie would be judging poodles and I hoped I would have an opportunity to see her in action.

Poodles were a popular breed, and there were a lot of them entered. Dixie had given me a crash course in conformation shows, which helped a bit, but there were still quite a few gaps in my understanding. I knew that most of the dogs entered were competing for points toward their AKC championship. To get the championship, each dog must acquire a total of fifteen points. The exact number of points awarded at each show differed by the breed. Popular breeds like poodles required more entries than less common breeds.

A parade of fluffy poodle puppies pranced by, and I smiled at the solid color fluff balls. I was engrossed in watching the various dogs.

"Enjoying the show?" Dixie asked.

I hadn't seen her approach. I clutched my chest and took several deep breaths. "You scared me. Aren't you supposed to be judging?"

She looked at her watch. "I've got about an hour before my trial."

Dixie was tall and thin. At nearly six feet barefoot, she was a presence to be reckoned with in pumps, especially with her big Dolly Parton hair and mass of jewelry. She was a Southern belle with all that the label entailed. She also had a heart the size of Tennessee and loved poodles. Today, her earrings and the scarf she stylishly wore around her neck declared her love of poodles for anyone who was in doubt.

"I don't understand how there are so many poodles competing."

Dixie smiled. "Well, poodles are popular, so there are usually quite a few in practically any competition, but this is a popular show and with so many dogs entered, you stand a real good chance of getting a major."

I must have looked as baffled as I felt because she chuckled.

She took a deep breath and went into her teaching mode where she spoke slowly to make sure I followed. "In order to get a championship, a dog must get at least two majors, which are wins of three, four, or five points awarded by at least three different judges."

"What determines the number of points?"

"The number of dogs competing. The greater the number of dogs competing, the greater the number of points. The maximum points you can win is five and there are a lot of poodles entered, so a win here will mean a five-point major." She looked at me. "You follow?"

I nodded.

"So, the males and females compete separately in seven different classes—Puppy, Twelve-to-Eighteen Months, Novice, Amateur-Owner Handler, by Exhibitor, American-Bred, and Open. Then, all the winners in their class will compete again to determine the best of the winners."

"Are the males and females still separated?"

She nodded. "Yep. Only the best male 'Winners Dog' and the best female 'Winners Bitch' receive championship points. The 'Winners Dog' and

'Winners Bitch' then compete with the champions for BEST OF BREED. At the end of the Best of Breed Competition, three awards are usually given: Best of Breed—the dog judged as the best in its breed category, Best of Winners—the dog judged as the better of the Winners Dog and Winners Bitch, and Best of Opposite Sex—the best dog that is the opposite sex to the Best of Breed winner."

"Wow!" My head was spinning.

"It's a lot, but the bottom line is there are a lot of poodles competing, and each day we go through the same thing. So the judges rotate to give us a bit of a break and to allow the dogs the chance to earn their championship points under different judges."

She gasped as a beautiful silver standard pranced by. "That is one beautiful bitch."

I'd long since stopped registering shock at hearing the word some used as a vulgarity when applied in its one true context. "How can you tell?" I stared at the silver dog. "I mean, she's beautiful, but what makes her stand out more than any of these others?"

Dixie smiled. "It's something about the bone structure, the way she carries herself, the line, and, ultimately, it's that certain….something that sets her apart." She shrugged. "You know how sometimes on those reality shows for singing or dancing the most technically talented person isn't always the person who wins?"

I nodded.

"It's the same thing. Sometimes there's just something about a dog that sets it apart." She shook her head. "You can't always put your finger on it, but there's just something special about some dogs and you know it when you see it."

We talked about poodles for a bit longer and watched a few rounds of judging. I told Dixie about my opportunity to go to the art auction. She clapped and nearly created a faux pas when she shouted, but her timing was excellent. Her reaction was simultaneous with the judge proclaiming the silver poodle Dixie liked as the winner, so her scream coincided with the thunderous applause and shouts from the audience. Dixie was one of the few people who knew how much I wanted to attend the auction, so her response made me feel great.

"I'm so glad for you, although I'm really sorry Jacob broke his ankle. I'll send him flowers." She pulled out her cell phone and left a note for herself. When she was done, she put her phone back in her pocket. "Now, when do you leave?"

"Tomorrow."

"What are you going to do with Aggie?"

I sighed. "I was thinking about boarding her."

"If Beau and I weren't going to Gatlinburg, you know I'd take her." She looked genuinely sad. "Maybe we can just have her stay with the girls. I'm sure Mike won't mind."

I laughed. "Your girls are two standard poodles."

She waved away my objection. "He loves Chyna and Leia. What's one more?"

"I appreciate the offer, but I don't think so."

Dixie protested, but I was firm. Eventually she realized I was sincere. "What about Red?"

"He's at that TBI workshop."

"Is he still incommunicado?"

I nodded. "No outside distractions. He gave me a number where I could reach him in case of emergency, but I don't think this qualifies."

Dixie hesitated a moment, but then she nodded. "You're right. I doubt seriously if those TBI guys would consider this an emergency." She smiled.

I pulled the brochure for Pet Haven from my purse. "Have you heard about this place?"

She took the brochure. "Oh yes. I know several people who board their dogs there. They asked me to come and do a demonstration, but I just haven't had the time. It's supposed to be very *exclusive*." She looked up from the brochure. "Television? Shiatsu massage?"

I nodded. "I met one of the owners yesterday. It sounds really fancy, but the one thing I liked was the pet cam." I pointed to it in the brochure. "I can go online and watch Aggie. If I have to leave her someplace, at least it will be nice to watch her."

"That is a plus." She folded the brochure and handed it back to me. "I haven't heard anything negative about them. I believe Monica Jill takes Jac there for doggie day care." She looked at her watch. "I still have time before I have to judge my first group. Let's run back to their booth and I'll grill the owner for you."

I was ecstatic that Dixie volunteered to go with me, so we hurried out to the vendor area.

Pet Haven's tent was as elegant as I remembered, but today, instead of Keri Lynn Simpson, a man was there. I almost didn't realize it wasn't her. They were both tall with a mane of blond hair. However, his hair was cut shorter. He turned and immediately flashed a smile, which made me wish I'd brought my sunglasses.

He started toward us but stopped a few feet before reaching us. After a long pause, he put his hand over his heart. "Be still my heart." He patted his chest and then walked up to us and took each of us by the hand. "Please forgive me, ladies, but it's not every day that angels descend from heaven." He sighed. "My name is Dallas Simpson. How can I serve you?"

Similar to Keri Lynn Simpson, Dallas Simpson was attractive. He was tall with chiseled good looks, which included a square jaw, cleft chin, and sparkling blue eyes. Unlike Keri Lynn, who was a natural beauty, Dallas's beauty was anything but natural. He was dark, due to a tan that had most likely come from a bottle or a spray can. His teeth were white, too white to be natural. His hair was too perfectly coiffed to be free of gel, with blond highlights that came from a bottle rather than the sun. He was dressed entirely in white and looked as though he'd just stepped off the cover of a men's fashion magazine. Everything about Dallas Simpson was packaged for maximum appeal.

Dixie and I both pulled our hands free, and I used all of my mental energy to stop myself from wiping my hand on my pants leg. My mind told me it was oily, even though I knew that wasn't the case.

"I'm Dixie Jefferson." Dixie took a step backward to regain a fraction of the personal space Dallas had encroached upon. "My friend Lilly is interested in boarding her dog, but we have some questions."

"Certainly." He smiled. "I'll be happy to answer any questions you have." He turned to the table to get one of the brochures, but Dixie stopped him.

"We already have the brochure, and Lilly talked to Keri Lynn yesterday." Dixie held up the brochure I'd given her earlier.

He nodded. "Keri Lynn's my wife."

"Yes, well, I don't have a lot of time, so let's get started." She then grilled Dallas Simpson. She questioned him about everything from the number of workers per dog, the amount of supervised versus unsupervised play my dog would get, as well as their methods for discipline. She got the name of the veterinarian they used in the event of emergencies and the names of three references. She pounded him with so many questions, I almost felt sorry for him…almost. When he'd answered everything to her satisfaction, she gave me a brief nod.

I noticed a bead of sweat had dripped down the side of Mr. Perfect's face, and his smile looked forced. "I just learned about a business trip I will need to make tomorrow, so I would like to make a reservation for my dog, Aggie."

Dallas Simpson took down my information and promised the best accommodations for Aggie.

He assured me I could drop Aggie off at any time, including tonight, but I wasn't ready to part with her quite that soon. Instead, I made arrangements to drop Aggie off at their facility early tomorrow morning. According to Dixie, that was a benefit, because most places wouldn't allow drop-off or pickup on Sunday.

When we left, I thought I noticed Dallas wiping his brow.

The rest of the afternoon went by far too quickly. I spent the majority of the time watching Dixie judging poodles. She looked confident and self-assured in the ring. She noted every aspect of each dog from the eyes to the tail. She looked at each dog's teeth and ran her hands through their elaborately cut coats. She took her time with each dog and watched them prance around the ring. She knew what she was looking for, and when the time came to pick a winner, she unwaveringly made her selection.

I left before the end of the trial because I needed to pack and I wanted to spend more time with Aggie. Back at the hotel, I took her for a long walk, careful not to let her roll in anything that would require another bath.

I packed, then ate Chinese takeout and watched a *Murder, She Wrote* marathon until I fell asleep. I woke once, when my leg was cramped, and realized Aggie had been using my knee as a pillow. It must have been a testament to how tired she was that she barely complained when I moved her to get up to answer the call of nature.

The next morning, I dressed and took Aggie out for her morning constitutional. She looked several times at the suitcase I put in the car, and I'd swear her eyes asked, *Where do you think you're going?* Dixie had warned me not to make a big deal of leaving because dogs picked up on our emotions. So I forced a smile and used my Lamaze breathing technique from childbirth to settle my nerves as I drove to Pet Haven.

Dallas Simpson had given me the address, and according to the directions on my phone, it wasn't far from my hotel. In fact, the entire ride took less than fifteen minutes.

Pet Haven Pet Resort and Doggie Day Care was a new building located a few miles off the next exit off the interstate. I followed an access road until I came to a large gated facility. There was an intercom, and I pushed the button as Dallas had instructed and gave my name. Aggie had been lounging on the back seat, but when I pulled up to the intercom, she immediately took her position at the window, the position she always used to garner a treat whenever I pulled up to a drive-thru window.

"Sorry, girl, this isn't a drive-thru."

Aggie wagged her tail expectantly as the gate opened and I pulled through.

She looked so disappointed when we didn't immediately stop at a window where food was provided that I reached into the glove box and pulled out a dog biscuit I kept for emergencies like this.

As soon as I pulled into a parking space, the front door to the building opened, and a young woman came out to the car to greet us. Initially, I thought it was the owner, Keri Lynn, but a closer look showed me I was mistaken.

"Hello, Mrs. Echosby."

I tried to hide my surprise. "Hello."

"I'm Heather." She beamed. "This must be Aggie." She reached into the car and petted Aggie, whose tail swung from side to side like the amped-up pendulum on a clock.

"Yes, this is Aggie."

"May I?" She held her hands out to lift her.

Aggie hurled her six-pound body at the strange woman and licked her face as though she was covered in hot dogs.

I got out of the car and followed them into the building.

"Oh my goodness, you're a lover, aren't you?" She struggled to talk without Aggie sticking her tongue in her mouth. "This must be hard to leave such a sweet little dog."

"It is. I've never boarded her before." I struggled to keep from grabbing Aggie back from her and giving her a hug. Instead, I found myself explaining about Jacob's broken ankle and the chance to go to Atlanta with my boss.

Heather winced. "A broken ankle sounds painful. I broke my foot when I was a teenager and had to get a metal plate. It still bothers me when the weather gets cold." She laughed. "The kids used to call me the Bionic Woman. That's why I named my dog, Steve...for Steve Austin."

I raised an eyebrow. "I'm surprised you know who they are. That show was a long time ago. You don't seem old enough to have watched that."

She laughed. "I used to watch a lot of old television shows with my memaw before she died."

I must have looked the surprise I felt because she laughed. "MeMaw was my grandmother. She raised me."

"I'm sorry."

She shrugged. "My parents died when I was young, so it was just MeMaw and me. If you don't know anything different, then you don't feel regret."

Inside, the building looked like a high-class hotel with high ceilings, marble floors, and a waterfall fountain on one wall. I looked around and could easily understand why the prices were as steep as they were. This was definitely a resort.

Heather went to a door at the back wall of the building and pushed a button. There was a buzz and then there was a click. She twisted the handle, opened the door, and held it open for me to precede her. "Dallas... ah, I mean, Mr. Simpson thought you might like a tour."

Inside the inner sanctum, I followed Heather down a hallway. To the right was a large glass wall where several dogs were running and playing. True to Dallas's word, there was a worker for each dog, making sure the play remained friendly.

"This is our doggie day care. Many of our guests come to play several days per week." She walked slowly, with Aggie cuddled up to her chest. She turned a corner, and we passed a grooming salon, the massage room, an indoor pool, and an acupuncture room. At the end of the hall was another door. There was a camera and a fingerprint scanner, which she used to gain admittance.

"Wow! That's pretty high-tech stuff."

She smiled and pointed to the cameras that discreetly lined the walls. "Dallas...ah...I mean Mr. Simpson takes great pride in providing the best security for your loved one."

We entered the boarding area, which was massive.

"These are our guest rooms." Heather led the way.

There were glass walls on either side of a long corridor. Walking down the halls, I could see into the "rooms." Each was indeed decorated in a different theme. The Paris Room had a mural of all of the tourist attractions of Paris, including the Eiffel Tower, Arc de Triomphe, and the Louvre Museum. The décor was pink and black with a fancy dog bed that matched the motif.

"As you can see, each suite is decorated to meet your pet's needs."

A Yorkshire terrier yipped at us from behind one of the glass walls.

We walked past rooms decorated like everything from a British castle to an Alpine ski chalet. At the end of the hall she stopped and opened the door. The theme was a log cabin. It included everything from a fake fireplace to a large faux bearskin rug. The cabin didn't represent my personal design aesthetic, but Aggie really seemed to love it. She nearly leapt out of Heather's arms when we entered. It might have had something to do with the large box of toys and treat box that was in the room. Aggie stood on her hind legs and pranced around in a circle like a ballerina.

"What's this?"

Heather smiled. "We like to welcome all of our special guests with a little gift. Dallas...ah...Mr. Simpson wanted to make sure Aggie had VIP treatment."

I opened the box. Inside was a blanket, a stuffed toy, and a treat shaped like a dog bone, which had Aggie barking and pawing at my hands. I turned to Heather. "I don't give—"

She held up a hand. "It's a homemade treat we make in house."

"In house?"

She nodded. "We have a commercial kitchen where we prepare special meals for some of our guests with dietary restrictions. Dallas...ah...Mr. Simpson has the chef make organic treats that are not only veterinarian-approved but safe for human consumption."

I raised an eyebrow. "You're kidding."

She shook her head. "Go ahead, take a bite."

I stared at the bone-shaped treat and then sniffed it. I contemplated taking a bite, but I couldn't get over the shape. Instead, I held it out to Aggie, who nearly snatched it out of my hand. She dragged the bone to the rug in front of the fake fireplace and lay down. The treat between her paws, she gnawed on it.

I stood, watching her for several moments. Aggie was so engrossed in her treat she didn't seem to care I was leaving. I picked her up, still clutching the treat, and gave her a hug. However, she wasn't the least bit interested. I put her down and she resumed her previous position, only this time she turned so her back was to me.

I slunk out of the room.

Heather followed me and turned to me once the door was closed. "We find the treat a good distraction for drop-offs." She looked at her watch, a cheap Mickey Mouse trinket with a bright neon-pink band. She frowned.

"Can you tell me the time?" She tapped the watch.

I looked at my phone. When I told her the time, we picked up the pace. She led me back down the hallway, then reached into her pocket and handed me a card. While we walked back the way we came, she explained, "This is a card with the important information, including our telephone number, the number of her suite, and directions for watching her on the pet cams."

When we were back in the lobby, I took care of the mundane information of checking Aggie in.

"You have great handwriting." I noticed her beautiful script.

She smiled. "Thank you. I used to be left-handed when I was younger and my handwriting was horrible."

"Used to be left-handed?"

She nodded. "Yeah, my teachers forced me to use my right hand." She shook her head. "Some superstitions about left-handed people being evil. When I was a kid, my teachers spanked me if I used my left hand for anything."

"That's horrible."

She shrugged. "Now I can't really use my left hand for much of anything."

I completed the forms with my vet information and my contact information and left a credit card for charges.

Later, I sat in the car and stared at the building. I felt like a mother who had dropped her infant off at day care for the first time. I was confident the staff would take good care of Aggie. Plus, I was only going to be gone for a few days. Aggie would have a great time. However, none of that prevented a tear from falling as I backed out of the parking lot and drove away. As I looked back at the building in my rearview mirror, a dark cloud rolled overhead and I couldn't get away from the feeling in the pit of my stomach that it was a bad sign.

Chapter 3

By the time I got on the interstate, excitement had drowned out the sadness. Once I arrived at the museum, where I'd agreed to meet Linda Kay, I was laughing at the memory of Aggie, sprawled out sphinx-like on a bear-skinned rug gnawing away at a huge dog-shaped treat that was nearly as long as she was.

I was the first to arrive and checked my watch. If I hurried, I could run over to Da Vinci's bakery and pick up coffee and some delicious treats for the ride. The bakery was just a block away from the museum, and I was lucky to get there when there wasn't the normal long line of customers. I recognized the young man behind the counter from my nearly daily visits since I'd discovered the bakery.

"Good morning. The usual?" Brad smiled.

"Not today." I explained I was taking a road trip with my boss and her husband and wanted a few goodies for the road.

He nodded and suggested a variety pack of pastries and a carton of coffee. He even threw in three travel mugs to help. Da Vinci's wasn't cheap, but it was well worth the price. So I paid and hurried back to the parking lot.

I didn't have long to wait. Linda Kay and her husband, Edward, pulled up next to me in a white SUV that made my heart contract with the tiniest bit of jealousy. When I saw Linda Kay's beautiful smile radiating at me from the front passenger seat window, I quickly squelched all jealous feelings and smiled back.

She lowered her window. "Good morning. Sorry we're a little late."

"No worries. You gave me time to pick up a little something for the trip." I got out of the car and retrieved the Da Vinci's container.

"Oh my goodness, you shouldn't have."

I passed the container to her through the window.

"But I'm really glad you did." She laughed.

Edward got out and walked around to help me with my luggage. I popped the back hatch of my SUV, and he reached in and got my suitcase. "Is this it?" He shot a glance at his wife. "Imagine that, only one suitcase." He turned away and winked at me.

Edward Weyman was a quiet, soft-spoken man. He wasn't tall, nor was he short. He wasn't fat or skinny. He was an average man of average height with an average-looking face. His brown eyes and wispy brown hair were also pretty average and nondescript. However, what set Edward Weyman apart was his heart. He was the kindest, most gentle soul of a man I'd ever met. I knew from Linda Kay he was retired from the post office. He had always been handy and had used a lot of those skills to help make their home handicap-accessible by building a ramp for Linda Kay's scooter, installing handrails, and retrofitting their kitchen so she could indulge in one of her favorite pastimes, cooking. Now he was fulfilling a lifelong passion and had started building custom furniture. Like me, Edward wasn't an employee of the museum, so I knew from doing the books, his expenses weren't covered. Nevertheless, I thought it showed how much he loved Linda Kay that he often traveled with his wife, especially for overnight stays, to help her with personal things and to make sure she was comfortable. Jacob said at one time Linda Kay had been more mobile and used crutches, but she was no longer able to do that and relied on her scooter much more. Jacob was an employee and had majored in art, so his trip would have been paid by the museum. He would not only be able to help Linda Kay with any work-related things, but he would also be able to lend his knowledge and expertise to her. Unfortunately, that was one area where I wouldn't be able to help. However, I was determined to do my best.

When I got into the back seat, I felt as though I was sitting in the lap of luxury. The saddle-brown quilted leather seat felt like butter and had charcoal piping and wood trim, which gave the vehicle an added layer of opulence.

"Nice car." I ran my hands over the seat.

"Thank you." Linda Kay handed me a coffee and extended the pastry box for me to make a selection. "We got a great deal on it."

"Our old car got damaged in a hailstorm." Edward backed out of the parking lot.

"We loved that car." Linda Kay took a bite of a cheese Danish and moaned.

Edward got us onto the interstate in a few short turns before reaching over and selecting a pastry from the box. "Totaled…"

"We were forced to get a new car and needed something big enough to accommodate my scooter." Linda Kay finished his sentences as a matter of practice acquired after three decades of marriage.

I had a great conversation with Linda Kay, with the occasional smart-alecky crack thrown in by Edward. When combined with the sensation of floating on clouds that riding in a luxury vehicle gave me, it was a quick and pleasant trip. The two-hour ride from Chattanooga to Atlanta flew by in record time. Even the normally paralyzing Atlanta traffic wasn't as torturously slow, and we actually continued to move. Although at times we crept along at a snail's pace, we continued to move. I thanked God multiple times for the commuter lane. The fact that today was Sunday also probably contributed a lot to our continued forward progress.

During the ride, Linda Kay filled me in on what to expect at the art auction, which I found fascinating. She likened the event to an upscale and refined sporting event akin to *The Hunger Games*. Art lovers, museum curators, and collectors vied for the finest works of art.

She passed to me the catalog the auction house had provided, and I flipped through the pages, marveling at the beautiful paintings, sculptures, glass works, and other objects. Linda Kay and Jacob had pored over the catalog for weeks prior to the auction, but since I wasn't expected to attend, I'd stuck to my ledgers.

"We don't have pockets deep enough to get the really fine pieces," Linda Kay said.

I gasped. "This says Leonardo da Vinci," I said in the quiet, reverential tone I reserved for church and funerals. "Seriously, they're auctioning a *real* Leonardo da Vinci?"

Linda Kay chuckled. "It's actually a newly discovered Leonardo. Experts are still debating the authenticity of the painting, but enough of them have signed off on it that it's finally getting acknowledged as the real thing." She shook her head. "The curators from the big museums will be bidding on that. Although I think it'll go to a private collector."

"Wow! I can't believe they're still finding paintings by Leonardo da Vinci after all this time." I paused to consider the idea that a masterpiece could lie around, undiscovered and unrecognized, for centuries. "Do you think it's real?"

I saw her shoulders rise in a shrug. Although I couldn't see her face, I knew the expression. "Beats me."

"Not likely," Edward mumbled as he skillfully changed lanes.

"Check out that pendant on page twenty-seven," Linda Kay said.

I flipped to the page and stared at a gold and enamel egg pendant. "A translucent mauve enamel divided by a chased laurel band within red and opaque white borders." I scanned the rest of the description. "Believed to be created circa eighteen ninety-five by Fabergé work master Alfred Thielemann." I looked up. "What's a Fabergé work master?"

"The House of Fabergé operated in the late nineteenth century, much like a McDonald's franchise today. When Carl Fabergé took over running the business in the late eighteen hundreds, things were going well. In fact, there was so much work the two Fabergé brothers couldn't keep up. So, they hired craftsmen...work masters, who owned their own workshops to produce the jewelry and art pieces they designed. The brothers provided sketches or models of what they wanted, but the craftsman did the actual work."

"You mean Fabergé didn't create their own artworks? Not even the Fabergé eggs?"

Linda Kay chuckled. "Probably not. Although Carl Fabergé was a highly trained craftsman, there's no proof he actually made anything." She took a peek at me in the rearview mirror and laughed. "Oh, my goodness. I'm sorry to burst your bubble."

"Well, if they didn't make them, why are they called Fabergé eggs?"

"The House of Fabergé designed them. The craftsmen were commissioned to execute their designs."

"Walt Disney didn't create most of the Disney films," Edward said.

"You're right. I guess I just envisioned Fabergé as this brilliant jeweler who designed those amazing eggs."

"He was a brilliant jeweler. However, he most likely didn't sit down and spend countless hours actually sculpting, soldering, and creating the eggs. It's known that two master workmen were responsible for creating most of the eggs, Michael Perkhin and a Finnish jeweler, Henrik Wigström."

"I feel like you've just told me there's no Santa Claus."

"Of course there's a Santa Claus. Don't let anyone tell you any differently." Linda Kay laughed. "Seriously, I hope I haven't ruined the art show for you."

"Oh no. Not at all." I shook off the disappointment I'd allowed to cloud my thoughts and flipped through the rest of the catalog. "Do you think you'll be able to get this pendant?"

"I'm hoping the big guns will be distracted by the da Vinci and the other sexier pieces during the evening sale tonight and then we'll just sneak in tomorrow at the day sale and snatch up a few bargains." She looked around the seat. "I did tell you to pack an evening dress, didn't I?"

I nodded. "I packed one, but it's been a long time since I've worn it. I hope it still fits."

Edward mumbled something about a "monkey suit" as he pulled off the interstate and up to the front of the Ritz-Carlton Hotel.

I stared at the large façade and said a silent prayer that I wouldn't say or do anything to embarrass myself or Linda Kay.

The marble floors, crystal chandeliers, and rich wood-paneled walls created an atmosphere of luxury, which would have normally made me uncomfortable. However, I found myself smiling at the thought that my dog was lounging in equally luxurious surroundings. My room was large, with a king-sized bed that felt huge for one person. I had a balcony that looked out on the city.

I had several hours before I needed to dress for the evening, so I pulled out my laptop and connected to the Pet Haven website. Aggie was stretched out on the bear-skinned rug in front of her fake fireplace, asleep with her head on a large stuffed bear. She looked peaceful and obviously unconcerned about me. The large bone treat was nearby, and I smiled at the corner of the treat that was missing. She might be small, but she was definitely determined.

Watching Aggie sleep made me drowsy. I decided to explore Atlanta rather than napping. I knew Linda Kay had scheduled a massage and Edward was planning to sit in the bar and watch some big college football game between the University of Georgia and Alabama.

According to the guidebook in my room, the hotel was only a half mile away from Centennial Olympic Park, the Georgia Aquarium, and a few other tourist attractions. I stopped at the concierge desk on my way out and got a map and confirmed my directions. Then I headed out for a quick look around.

Despite the fact that it was the middle of the winter, the weather in Atlanta was still warm. I walked to Centennial Olympic Park and watched the water shoot up from the Olympic rings. My timing was great, and I was able to watch one of the four Fountain of Rings shows, where the fountains were synchronized to familiar music and included lighting and sound effects. The show was spectacular, and I found myself applauding with the other spectators when it was over. In addition to the map, the concierge had also given me a brochure about the park, which included a link to their mobile website. The website had an audio tour, which I listened to as I strolled. I learned about the park's history and the 1996 Olympic Games, which the city of Atlanta had hosted. In addition to the history, I also learned about the architecture and culture of the city through the music and even a trivia game. The twenty-one-acre park was massive. Too massive to explore completely. So I took a few pictures with my cell phone and made a mental promise to return in the spring or summer. Visiting the aquarium would have to wait too. Hopefully, I'd have time tomorrow to explore more.

I made my way back to the hotel in time for tea on the mezzanine, another item my in-room brochure alerted me to try. It wasn't quite the same as the high teas Dixie and I experienced when we spent a semester abroad in college. However, it was a wonderful, indulgent experience I thoroughly enjoyed. Sterling silver tea strainers and bone china cups gave the event a feeling of elegance. Champagne was an American addition that lent to the special feel. In addition to the tea, the hotel served slices of seeded tea cakes, scones, and sandwiches with salmon and caviar, certainly a step up from the cucumber sandwiches I'd had in England.

After tea, I went to my room and took a quick nap before showering and dressing for dinner. Linda Kay and Edward had arranged to meet me for cocktails at six, by which time I was refreshed and excited. It wasn't every day I got to dress up in fancy evening wear and mingle with tuxedo-clad art experts.

Linda Kay was dressed in a black full-length evening dress with an elegant silver brocade jacket. From under her scooter, one silver shoe rested. Linda Kay only had one leg, but she never let that hinder her from doing whatever she chose, including kickboxing classes or tai chi. I had yet to muster up the courage to ask how she managed the kickboxing, but perhaps the occasion would present itself for me to ask.

Edward stood nearby in the standard black tuxedo that all of the men had donned. His eyes darted around the room like a caged animal's, and he tugged at his shirt collar so frequently, Linda Kay swatted his hand.

"Good evening. You two look wonderful," I said.

"We clean up pretty nice, don't we?" Linda Kay smiled. "Now, if Edward will stop tugging at his collar, folks might think we belong here."

Edward took a sip of his drink and mumbled something about "feeling like a waiter."

Linda Kay smiled at me. "Now, you look absolutely gorgeous in that dress. I'll bet Red would fall on his knees if he saw you in that."

Heat rose to my face. "I bought this dress years ago to wear to a fancy Christmas Eve party in Lighthouse Dunes, but Albert got shingles and we weren't able to go." I stared at the dress, which was also black. It was a fitted black velour dress with a bateau neckline and long sleeves. At the top of each shoulder was white sheer fabric that flowed on each side of a plunging deep V on the back that went almost to my waist, where it ended in a large bow. In contrast to the conservative front, the back also had a slit that went farther than my Midwestern sensibilities would have liked. In fact, I'd considered having the slit reduced. However, I found the slit made it possible for me to not only walk without shuffling like Morticia Addams, but it also allowed me to lift my leg enough to get in and out of the car.

Linda Kay grinned. "I haven't known you long, but this dress is beautiful, and I just can't imagine …"

I laughed. "You can't picture a conservative CPA like me wearing it?"

She laughed. "Well, it doesn't seem like something you'd pick."

"Normally, I wouldn't have worn anything quite this daring." I explained how I'd taken the train to Chicago and my daughter, Stephanie, and I had gone shopping to find something to wear to the party. We'd gone to several stores with no luck. Before giving up, Stephanie insisted we try Neiman Marcus on Michigan Avenue. I was certain I couldn't afford an umbrella in the store, but I was surprised when she discovered the designer dress on a clearance rack. It had been marked down multiple times and was now less than fifty dollars.

Linda Kay laughed. "Now, that sounds like you."

Edward returned with a glass of champagne for each of us. We talked and Linda Kay smiled and chatted with art associates who came up to talk to her. Eventually, it was time for dinner and we went into the dining room.

Dinner was delicious, and I ate more than I should, but I promised myself I'd walk it off tomorrow in the aquarium. Afterward, we drank coffee until it was time for Linda Kay to pick up her paddle and make her way to the evening show in the hotel's ballroom.

The outskirts of the room showcased many of the art exhibits up for bid. Paintings, objets d'art, and sculptures were positioned to provide easy viewing, but limited access. The center front of the room held a stage and a podium, and there were more than a hundred chairs facing the stage. On one side was a raised platform with seats and telephones.

At the podium, a man announced the auction would be starting soon, and all of the guests took their seats for the show.

My first auction felt more like interactive theater. The host, an apparently well-known art expert who'd flown over from Britain, joked and entertained the crowd. Unlike the typical fast-paced rhythmic chanting I'd seen at auctions at the fairgrounds in Indiana, art auctioneers spoke in a slow, deliberate manner. Instead of bidders yelling their price, they raised a small white paddle with a number on it. It was classy and distinguished, and I was enthralled as I tried to follow the bidding.

"What's with the phones?" I whispered to Linda Kay.

She glanced to the side. "Those are people who are calling in their bids."

When the evening sale was over, everyone applauded and then made their way out of the room.

"Wow. I'm tired just watching all of that. Will tomorrow be the same?"

"The basics of how things work is the same. However, there won't be nearly as many people and prices won't be as high."

We said our good nights and made arrangements to meet for breakfast the next morning.

In my room, I got ready for bed and marveled at the turn my life had taken. Just a few short months ago I was trying to cope with the end of my marriage. When my husband left me for a younger woman, I thought my life was over. Over time, I realized my marriage had ended long before Albert walked out. I looked out of my window on the city lights of Atlanta. I opened the balcony door, stepped outside, and listened to the buzz of the lights and conversations from people moving about, despite the late hour. There was an energy to the city that crackled like static electricity. For a moment, my thoughts took me back to a late-night train ride from Chicago to Lighthouse Dunes, where I met a woman who changed my life. Miss Florrie was a kind African American woman who helped me put things in perspective. My brief conversation with her helped me realize I'd been holding on to a life I no longer wanted. She gave me the courage to let go of the past and try to find my "happy place." Now, here I was attending an art auction six hundred miles away from Lighthouse Dunes, Indiana. I was working at a job I loved. I was buying a house. I had friends and was starting a relationship with a man who was kind and genuinely seemed to care. It was early days yet, but I was excited to see where things might lead. I even had a dog, something I'd always wanted but Albert had vetoed. Thoughts of Aggie made me smile.

I heard a loud clap of thunder, and lightning flashed across the sky. A light rain started to fall, and I went inside. I checked the clock. It was late, but I could still go online and watch Aggie for a few minutes on the pet cam before I went to bed.

I was still smiling when I pulled up my laptop and navigated to Pet Haven's website. I could hear the storm getting louder, and the Internet site that had been clear earlier in the day was staticky and slower tonight. I finally caught a glimpse of Aggie. She had moved from the bear-skinned rug to the cot, which was littered with stuffed animals. I was just about to turn off the screen when it flickered and then jumped to a view of one of the other cameras. I clicked around the menu on several links, which switched from one room to another in search of the link that would take me back to Aggie. Just about to give up, I clicked on a link that showed a woman spraying down the outside area of the kennels. It appeared to be raining there too, but the kennel area was covered. I squinted to make out who the woman was. It looked like the owner, Keri Lynn Simpson. She wore a yellow rain slicker and boots. I was glad to see Pet Haven was true to their brochures and cleaned every night. Her back was to the camera. She must have gotten a call because she moved the hose to her left hand and pulled out her cell phone. She glanced at the phone and then returned it to her pocket.

I was just about to shut down when a shadow approached her from the back. That was when I saw a man's arm reach around and grab her from the back. He put his hands around her neck and squeezed.

She dropped the hose and clawed at the man's arms and face, but it was too little, too late.

She slid to the ground.

What did I just see? What just happened?

Thunder clapped, and my screen went black.

Chapter 4

I sat in stunned silence for several moments. I paced while I tried to wrap my head around what I'd just seen. It wasn't until I picked up my cell phone and tried to dial Red's number that I noticed my hands were shaking. It took several tries before my fingers managed to hit the right numbers.

The phone rang so long I started to hang up, unsure if I'd dialed the right number.

Eventually, someone answered, but I didn't recognize the voice. "Hello."

"I need to get in touch with Red...ah, I mean Dennis Olson," I stammered.

"Who's calling?"

"Tell him it's Lilly."

There was a long pause. "Hold on."

I heard grunting, shuffling, and the squeaking of a cot. Eventually, I heard footsteps.

"Lilly? Are you okay? What's happened?" He fired questions at me with machine-gun speed.

"I'm fine. I just—"

"What happened?"

"I saw someone get murdered."

There was a pregnant pause. "Murdered? Are you okay? Did you call the police?"

"No, I haven't called anyone, but you."

"I'm not in Chattanooga, and it'll take me at least an hour to get there, but you need to call the police."

"I'm not in Chattanooga either. I'm—"

"Where are you?"

I knew it was concern for my safety, but if he kept interrupting me, I'd never get this out. "I'm in Atlanta. Red, I need you to listen." I explained about the art auction in Atlanta and the pet cams at Pet Haven as quickly as I could. He listened in silence. When I was finished, I took a deep breath.

"Are you sure she's dead?"

"I'm pretty sure. She slumped to the ground, and…it was awful." I shuddered at the memory.

"What do you see on the camera now? Is she still there?"

I looked at my laptop, which was still black. "I don't know. The storm made the screen staticky and the picture went black."

"Okay. I need you to call this number." He rattled off a number and I grabbed a pen and paper from the desk and wrote it down. He repeated the number. "Got it?"

"Yes, but what is this?"

"It's the number for the Chattanooga Police, homicide division." He told me what to say and I wrote down the key phrases. "Tell the detective that you've notified TBI and I'll be there in an hour." He paused. "You got it?"

I nodded, forgetting he couldn't see me.

"Lilly?"

"Oh, I'm sorry. I'm just so flustered. Do you think I should ask Edward to take me home early?" I hated to ruin the auction for Linda Kay, but surely murder took precedence.

"No. You stay where you are. I'll call you in a few hours and let you know what we find." He hesitated. "Okay?"

"Okay." I released a heavy breath. "Red…thank you."

I could hear the smile in his voice. "You're welcome."

Not surprisingly, I wasn't able to sleep after all that excitement. The storm continued into the early morning before it moved on. I tried several times to reconnect to the Internet, but the service was down.

Three hours later, my phone rang and I jumped.

"Red?"

"Yeah, it's me. I'm here with Officer Lewis." He sounded tired, and I felt bad for waking him and causing him to drive through the night; however, the poor woman who'd been murdered deserved to be treated better. She deserved better than to be brutally murdered as she was. Besides, I knew, from reading and watching mysteries, the sooner the police were brought in to investigate, the more likely they were to catch the killer.

"Did you find her? Was the killer still there? Did you catch him?" It was my turn to machine gun–fire questions, and at the speed of sound. When I finally stopped to catch a breath, I noticed the line was quiet. "Red, are you still there?"

He sighed. "Yeah, I'm here."

I waited.

After a long pause, he sighed again. "Lilly, we didn't find anyone."

"You mean the killer got away?"

"No, I mean we didn't find anything. We've searched every inch of the facility and there's no body."

I was stunned into silence. When my brain started working again, I said, "He must have gotten rid of the body."

"Did you see the man's face?"

"Well, no...but I'm pretty sure it was the owner, Dallas Simpson."

"Why?" He paused. "If you didn't see his face, what was it you saw that made you believe it was Dallas Simpson?"

"Well..." I thought back to what I'd seen. "It was a man. Who else could it have been at that time of night?"

"But if you didn't see his face, what makes you think it was this particular man?"

I was confused, and my brain wasn't functioning on all cylinders. Red was being cautious with his words, and there was something in his questions that gave me pause. "You don't believe me?"

"I didn't say that."

"You didn't have to." I was hurt, probably another result of my lack of sleep and the trauma of the past few hours. "I'm not crazy."

"No one said—"

"I know what I saw."

"I'm sure you saw something, but—"

"Is Keri Lynn Simpson there? Did you see her?"

"No. She's away at a dog show, but we spoke to her on the phone."

That left me stumped for a few seconds. "If you didn't see her, how do you know it was really her?"

He sighed.

"You know what, just forget it. I'm sorry I bothered you." I hung up.

My phone rang almost immediately, but Red's face popped up on the screen and I turned it off. I was behaving childishly, but I couldn't stop myself. I paced around the room and tried to gather my thoughts. Obviously, Dallas Simpson had hidden the body somewhere. "That explains why they didn't find the body," I muttered aloud as I paced. "Surely Red must have thought of that." I glanced at myself in the mirror over the dresser as I paced. That was when I realized I was crying.

I stopped and stared at what was looking back at me. Unlike actresses on television, I lacked the skill to cry and still look beautiful. My eyes were red and puffy, and I looked like a hot mess.

I looked at the clock. It was almost five, but I might as well get dressed. I needed a hot shower and plenty of coffee.

The bathroom wasn't a large room; it had nice finishes, which made the room feel opulent. I turned on the shower. The key element for me with any shower was the water pressure. The shower at the Ritz didn't disappoint. The water got steamy hot, and the water pressure pelted my skin with force. I didn't feel like I needed to hold on to the handrail to prevent being blown away, but I was pleasantly surprised at the spray. I stayed in the shower quite some time. The water helped my outer being as well as my emotional state. I knew Red was only doing his job. However, the fact that he didn't believe me still hurt. How could we build a relationship if we didn't have the single most important thing...trust? Trust was the foundation that everything else was built on. Without that, we didn't stand a chance. Months of analyzing my own failed marriage had helped me come to that realization. It wasn't the fact he'd cheated and been unfaithful. It was the fact he'd demonstrated he couldn't be trusted.

By the time I got out of the shower, my skin was pink and a little sore from the pounding from the shower, and I had a headache from crying. However, I was done. Miss Florrie had been right when she told me, "Tears are a precious commodity." She also said, "Ain't *no* man worth crying over." I pulled myself together. I knew that without trust, Red and I didn't have a future together, and I was too old to waste my time with someone who wasn't in this for the long haul. The next time I saw him, I would end the relationship.

I got dressed and applied makeup to try to hide the damage of a sleepless night and a morning spent crying. Then I went downstairs for coffee. I still had a couple of hours before I was scheduled to meet Linda Kay and Edward for breakfast. I grabbed a pen and notebook from my computer bag. Ending my relationship with Red wasn't the only decision I'd made in the shower. Just because someone didn't believe in me didn't change the facts. I'd seen someone murder another human being. Regardless of who she was or what she'd done, no person deserved to have her life snuffed out in such a way. That poor young woman was someone's daughter. I couldn't imagine how I'd feel if something like that happened to Stephanie or David. I might not have been able to prevent her murder, but the least I could do was try to make sure her murderer didn't get away scot-free. I was going to find her killer and bring him to justice.

Chapter 5

The hotel dining room had just opened. In fact, there was only one other person in the room when I arrived, so I had my pick of seating. I chose a table near the front window and ordered coffee. It looked like I was going to need a lot of it to stave off a pounding headache and convince my body I didn't need sleep.

The smell of bacon wafted from the kitchen and my stomach growled. My original intention had been to subsist on coffee until Linda Kay and Edward arrived. However, I switched to a new plan, which included bacon, eggs, and toast, and, of course, coffee now rather than later.

It didn't take long for them to prepare my breakfast. Everything was cooked perfectly, and there was even a small bowl of fruit. I ate quickly and washed everything down with coffee. When my hunger was sated, I pulled out my notebook and wrote down what I knew. After about ten minutes, what I knew wasn't much. I knew Keri Lynn and Dallas Simpson owned Pet Haven Pet Resort and Doggie Day Care. I knew a lady named Heather worked at the spa. I knew a woman wearing a yellow rain slicker and boots was rinsing out the kennel area last night. A man came up behind her and killed her. I also knew that by the time the police arrived, the killer had removed the body.

I tapped my pen on the table. "Surely there's got to be something else?"

My waiter was lingering nearby when I started muttering to myself, and he hurried over to see what I needed. I didn't think admitting I had been talking to myself instilled confidence in my waiter, who smiled and then rushed away, glancing back over his shoulder at me.

I took out my phone and turned it back on. I had twenty missed calls from Red and at least ten messages, but I didn't bother to listen to them. Instead, I got on the Internet and searched for information on Keri Lynn and Dallas Simpson. I found their names in connection with Pet Haven, plus there were several sites that promised to give me additional information for a fee, which I passed on.

I got lost in the sea of Internet searches and was surprised when I looked up and saw Linda Kay and Edward.

"Earth to Lilly." Linda Kay smiled as she motored up to one of the empty spots at the table.

"Sorry. I was absorbed." I put my phone down.

Edward pulled out a chair, sat down, and immediately poured Linda Kay a cup of coffee from the pot on the table, then poured one for himself.

"What's wrong?" Linda Kay sipped her coffee.

"Nothing."

She raised an eyebrow and stared. "I can tell by your eyes that something is wrong. Is it the children? Are Stephanie and David okay?"

"Everyone's fine."

"Don't tell me something happened to Aggie?"

I sighed. She was going to get it out of me one way or another, so I might as well come clean and tell her.

The waiter showed up and both Linda Kay and Edward ordered.

I waited until they were done and the waiter had gone to put in their orders before I started. I told them what I saw on the pet cam and also about Red's reaction.

They both listened to my tale with few interruptions. At times, Linda Kay shook her head and expressed shock and concern, especially when I described the murder. In fact, Linda Kay reached out a hand to comfort me.

By the time I'd finished telling my version of events, the waiter returned with their plates. They asked a few questions while they ate. I drank so much coffee I felt like I was going to float away. So I excused myself and went to find a nearby bathroom.

When I returned, I was stunned to see Red at the table. He stood when I arrived.

"What are you doing here?" I held my breath and whispered, "Aggie."

"Aggie's fine. I saw her a few hours ago."

I released the breath I'd been holding and tried to will my heart to slow down.

Red was about five ten, stocky, and rock solid. His short buzz cut proclaimed he'd been in the military. The scar that went down the right side of his face and something in the back of his dark eyes indicated he'd not only seen combat but had grappled with evil that would have crippled most humans.

"We need to talk." His eyes were bloodshot, and a five-o'clock shadow coated his face. His clothes were wrinkled and rumpled, and I could tell he'd had about as much sleep as I had.

"I don't want to talk to you right now."

"I gathered as much when you hung up on me and refused to take any of my calls." His voice sounded tired.

I looked over at Linda Kay and Edward. "I'm working. I'm going to a day show in"—I glanced at my watch—"less than thirty minutes."

"Oh, that's okay. You two should talk." Linda Kay smiled her gracious Southern lady smile. "I've got my paddle already, so I'm all set. Why don't you two run up to your room and have a chat and you can join me when you're done." She winked. "No hurry."

"But—"

"Good idea." Red grabbed me by the elbow. "It was nice seeing you both, again." He firmly but gently escorted me toward the door.

I sighed. I needed to talk to him sooner or later. I had hoped I would have more time to get my thoughts together. Unfortunately, his driving two hours during the middle of the night to Atlanta meant this conversation was going to happen much sooner. We walked in silence to the elevator. At the elevator, he held the door while I entered and pressed the button for my floor. When the elevator stopped, he let me exit first and followed me to my room. During the elevator ride, I made up my mind. No point in delaying. I needed to rip the Band-Aid off and just tell him. I opened the door to the room and he followed me inside.

When the door closed, I took a deep breath and then turned to face him. I opened my mouth, but the look on his face froze the words on my lips.

Red had learned over time to hide his emotions. In the short time I'd known him, I knew he rarely showed his feelings. However, for one unguarded moment, I saw behind the barrier. For a split second, I saw hurt.

He blinked, and the veil was back in place. He ran his hand through his hair. "Talk to me."

I took a deep breath. Everything had seemed so clear earlier. "I don't think we should see each other anymore."

"Why?"

"Because you don't trust me. We can't have a relationship without trust, and it was clear you didn't believe me."

"I never said I didn't believe you."

His words caught me by surprise. "Well, you sounded like you didn't believe me."

He sighed. "Lilly, I wouldn't have driven an hour to Pet Haven in the middle of the night if I didn't believe you. I wouldn't have searched that place with a fine-toothed comb or forced Officer Lewis to send a forensic team to go over the place if I hadn't believed you."

"But you…well, it sounded like you were questioning whether or not I saw what I said I saw."

He sighed. "That's my job. I have to ask questions to make sure witnesses are accurate." He smirked. "It's part of the training. We ask questions over and over in different ways. Sometimes people say things or remember things when a question is worded differently." He sighed. "It doesn't mean I don't believe you or that I don't trust you." He took a step toward me so we were inches apart. "I certainly wouldn't have driven two hours through the night to talk to you if I didn't trust you or care deeply for you."

This time when I looked into his eyes, I saw something entirely different and I melted.

He pulled me into his arms and kissed me, slowly and passionately. After an hour—or maybe it was a few minutes—I'd lost all sense of time, we came up for air.

I stroked his chin. "You need to shave."

He laughed and rubbed the stubble. "Sorry." He took a deep breath and paused. He looked as though he was searching for the right words. "Look, I'm not great at relationships. Communication isn't my strong point. When you strip away the fancy TBI title, I'm a cop. I didn't graduate from a fancy college. I'm pretty basic. Despite my mom and five older sisters' best intentions, I suck at talking about my feelings. I'm just a guy, and if we're going to try and make this work…" He raised an eyebrow. "You do want to make this work?"

I nodded.

He released a breath. "Good. Then I'm going to need you to help me out. If I'm being insensitive, I just need you to tell me straight. Don't assume I know what you're thinking or feeling, because I don't even know what I'm feeling most of the time."

I smiled and released a breath. "Okay."

He pulled me close and placed his head on mine. He lifted my chin and stared in my eyes. "Next time can we talk, please?"

"You're right. I shouldn't have gotten so angry. I shouldn't have hung up on you. It's just…trust is really important, and when I felt like you didn't believe me, it brought back all of my feelings of insecurity from Albert."

He wrapped his arms tightly around me. "I'm not Albert," he whispered. "I'm not saying I'll do everything right, but could you give me a chance?"

"I'm sorry. It's just that girl…she reminded me of Stephanie…" I laid my head on his shoulder and wept.

"Now I see, said the blind man."

We stood there for a few minutes. When the tears stopped, I pulled away and he handed me a handkerchief.

I dried my eyes and then blew my nose. "I must look horrible."

He shook his head. "You look beautiful to me."

I smiled. "Liar."

"That's my story and I'm sticking to it. My sisters did teach me the right answer to that question," he jested.

I gave him a playful punch.

He laughed and stifled a yawn.

"Sorry." He yawned again, but this time he wasn't able to suppress it. This time when I looked in his eyes, I saw weariness.

"You must be exhausted."

He protested, but the strain was obvious.

"Look, I need to go to the auction. Why don't you get some sleep here in my room? Linda Kay said we'll break for lunch around noon. If you're feeling up to it, you can join us for lunch."

For a moment, I thought he would object, but fatigue won out and he sat on the edge of the bed.

I went to the bathroom and replaced the makeup I'd just shed. I noticed my eyes were brighter, and for some reason, I couldn't stop grinning. I gave myself a final look in the mirror. I left the spare room key on the dresser, then placed the Do Not Disturb sign on the door and left him in the room. I went downstairs to join Linda Kay in the ballroom with a pep in my step and a smile on my face.

I found Linda Kay quite easily. There were few spots where her scooter would fit comfortably and where she would be easily visible to the auctioneer.

She had saved a seat between her and Edward. I sidled past her and sat down.

She looked at me. "You look happy."

I reached over and gave her hand a quick squeeze. "We're okay."

"Good. I'm so happy." She beamed. "I was afraid you were going to quit. You looked so angry when I encouraged you two to talk."

I smiled. "You're a wise woman."

"And Red is a good man," she added.

Edward nodded and mumbled, "Good man."

"He drove all this way to make things right. That proves he really cares." Linda Kay patted my knee. "I like him."

I smiled. "I like him too."

The auctioneer pounded his gavel, and the auction got underway. The day show wasn't nearly as elegant or exciting as the night show had been. The objects bid on were smaller, less well-known, and a lot less expensive. Linda Kay got the egg pendant she wanted, along with several other pieces, including two paintings, a vase, a book of poetry, and a clock. We broke for lunch, and Linda Kay was ecstatic.

I rushed up to the room. Red was sound asleep. At some point, he had brought up a duffel bag, which puzzled me a bit until I remembered he must have taken it to his secret TBI training. I hurried out of the room, careful not to wake him, and went downstairs.

Linda Kay, Edward, and I ate lunch in the dining room.

"I can't believe I got everything on my list," Linda Kay said.

"I can understand why you wanted the pendant, considering it's associated with Fabergé, but why did you want the other things?"

"The pendant was associated with Fabergé, but that's not why I wanted it." She took a sip of sweet tea. "I wanted it because we believe there's a connection between the Hopewells and Thielemann."

"Really?" I ate a spoonful of my sea crab cream sherry-infused soup and tried to contain a moan. I must not have done a good job because when I opened my eyes, Linda Kay and Edward were both laughing.

"I'm sorry, but this soup is the most delicious thing I've ever tasted. I'm so glad you suggested this."

Linda Kay waved her hand. "Honey, I wish I could order a bathtub full of the stuff and swim in it."

Edward shook his head, but his lips twitched as he tried to keep from smiling.

After a few minutes, Linda Kay put down her spoon. "Now, where was I?"

"You were saying you believe there's a connection between the Hopewells and Alfred Thielemann."

She took a bite of the chive cheese biscuits that were served with the soup. "Well, about a year ago, Jacob was looking for something in the attic of the Hopewell Mansion."

The Hopewells were a prominent family in Chattanooga at the turn of the twentieth century. I'd learned that Ulysses Hopewell was a tycoon who made a ton of money and built a big mansion on the bluffs in Chattanooga. His wife, Sarah Jane, was a socialite who loved art. After her husband died, she became a well-known art patron and founded the Hopewell Museum and Trust, which established the Chattanooga Museum of Art. The Edwardian-style mansion had been home to Ulysses and Sarah Jane and their eight children. Eventually, the family died out and the mansion was left to the trust as a museum. The main building was built later to house the great collection that Sarah Jane had amassed.

"Well, Jacob found some old diaries Sarah Jane had written, along with some pictures."

"Don't tell me. Sarah Jane and Alfred Thielemann were secret lovers, and he made the egg pendant for her as a token of his undying love and devotion, right?"

Linda Kay laughed. "Nothing quite that juicy, I'm afraid." She chuckled. "Although it does look as though Sarah Jane commissioned a few pieces of jewelry from Fabergé as a wedding gift for her daughter, Ruby."

"Ruby?"

She nodded. "There were newspaper clippings of the wedding announcement and everything, but the wedding never took place."

"What happened?"

"Jacob is still reading through the diaries. There are a lot of them, and the paper is old and the writing faint, but best we can tell, Ruby's intended died."

I put down my spoon. "How sad. Ruby must have been heartbroken."

"Sadly, not uncommon." She took a sip of her tea. "Medical science wasn't very good back then."

"Leeches and bloodletting were common practices," Edward murmured.

Linda Kay nodded. "They even gave patients cocaine for pain relief." She shook her head. "Her fiancé didn't die from sickness or disease, and I don't know if Ruby was that broken up about his death."

I must have looked shocked because she chuckled. "Don't look so shocked. From everything we can find, Sarah Jane was trying to make a good match for her daughter. Back then it was more important to make a *good* match than it was to make a *love* match. Feelings were rarely a consideration."

"But the Hopewells had money. They didn't need to find a wealthy husband to take care of their daughter," I said.

"True, but young ladies were *expected* to get married and have babies. Based on the pictures, Ruby wasn't exactly a raging beauty."

I frowned. "Was she ugly?"

Linda Kay laughed. "Not ugly, but maybe a little...plain." She shrugged. "Anyway, it looks like Sarah Jane was interested in prestige and...titles."

"Titles? Like, Mrs. Ruby Somebody-Or-Other?"

She shook her head. "More like, Lady Ruby Somebody-Or-Other."

"Oh, that kind of title. You mean Sarah Jane wanted to marry Ruby to some British aristocrat, like Winston Churchill's mother, Jennie Jerome?"

She nodded. "That's what it looks like, although Randolph was the third son and didn't inherit money or the title Duke of Marlborough. There are several letters that were tucked into the diary that Jacob read that indicated Sarah Jane had reached out to a matchmaker and arranged a marriage between Ruby and some broke but titled member of the British aristocracy."

I was barely able to hide my surprise. "That's amazing. So, what happened?"

"The young man, an earl, was supposed to come to the United States to meet the family, but...unfortunately, his ship sank." She paused and looked excited.

I waited for several seconds before the implication of what she was saying hit me. I stared for several seconds. "No way."

She nodded.

Edward stared from me to Linda Kay. "What?"

"He booked passage on an ocean liner." She smiled. "He left Southampton on April tenth, nineteen twelve, onboard the..."

"*Titanic*," we both said together.

Linda Kay nodded. She was silent a few moments. "Based on the diaries, it looks like some of the jewels and trinkets Sarah Jane commissioned from Fabergé were created by Alfred Thielemann." She sipped her tea. "We showed the diaries and letters to the chairman of the trust. Some of the descriptions fit. We may never be able to prove these are the exact objects, but they're good pieces and we can certainly weave an interesting story for a display in April about the tragic lost love affair around the anniversary of the *Titanic*."

I frowned. "Sounds a bit gruesome."

"I know, but the chairman loved it and agreed to let me purchase the items." She gave a smug smile. "Don't worry. Jacob will make the display amazing. He has such a wonderful eye for art."

We talked about the other pieces Linda Kay purchased, but none held the same allure as the lost love and the romanticism of the *Titanic*. We finished eating and returned for the last part of the auction.

There weren't any other items that Linda Kay was specifically interested in, so after an hour, we left.

"Why don't you go up and check on your young man? You two should go out and explore Atlanta."

"Are you sure?" I asked.

"Of course. I want to go to the Atlanta Botanical Garden. There's a Dale Chihuly exhibit going on, and I don't intend to miss it."

Dale Chihuly was a world-famous glass artist, and Linda Kay was a big fan of his work. The museum had a couple of smaller pieces, but I had heard about his wonderful glass gardens. Under different circumstances, I would have tagged along to the botanical garden. However, I knew I should spend some time with Red, especially since he'd traveled so far.

"Well, speak of the devil." Linda Kay smiled.

I turned to see what she was smiling at just as Red walked up to me. "You look better. Did you sleep well?"

"I feel much better, and yes, I did sleep well." He rubbed his chin.

I turned to hide the smile that threatened to form on my lips as I remembered how much his stubble scratched.

"Edward and I are going to check out an exhibit at the botanical gardens, but Lilly is free if you two want to go exploring." She gave a wicked smile and winked at Red.

He chuckled. "I'd like to stay, but unfortunately I need to head back to Chattanooga." He looked at his watch. "I have about an hour or two, but then I want to get out of the city before the rush hour traffic."

"So soon?" I struggled to keep the disappointment out of my voice.

"Sorry."

"You know, I'm pretty much done with all of the items I planned to buy." Linda Kay turned to me. "If you want to ride back to Chattanooga with Mr. Olson tonight, rather than waiting until tomorrow morning, that's fine too."

I looked from Red to Linda Kay, trying to read both of their faces. I wasn't sure if Red would want me to ride back with him or if he wanted to be alone. His face didn't give me any clues to his feelings. Linda Kay seemed genuinely sincere.

I turned to her. "Are you sure?"

She waved and *tsk*ed. "Of course. I'm retiring my paddle. We'll be leaving first thing tomorrow, once I confirm the shipping arrangements."

I turned to Red. "How about you?"

"Sure. It's fine with me."

I didn't detect any hesitation from him.

"Plus, you can go and pick up your baby." Linda Kay sealed the deal when she mentioned Aggie.

Decision made, I hurried upstairs and quickly packed while Red waited patiently. When I was ready, he took both of our bags down to his car and I left my room keys in an envelope at the front desk. I felt guilty about the museum paying for my room, but Linda Kay had gotten the board chairman's approval, so she took care of all of the charges.

Red pulled up in front of the hotel and waited for me. When I came out of the hotel, he jumped out of the car and made it around to open the door for me. I loved that he did old-fashioned things like opening doors.

It took longer for me to pack than I anticipated, and we didn't make it out of town before rush hour traffic. We didn't talk much while he concentrated on getting on the interstate, weaving in and out of the congestion of rush hour traffic, road construction, and disabled vehicles. After about thirty minutes, the traffic thinned out, and his grip on the steering wheel relaxed.

"Better now?" I asked.

He glanced at me. "Sorry. I tend to get a bit tense when I have to navigate through this city."

"I think that's why Linda Kay and Edward are leaving tomorrow. They timed their trip to avoid the worst of the traffic."

"Are you hungry?"

I did a quick self-assessment. "Not really, but I had lunch. Are you?"

"I am, but I can wait until we get back to Chattanooga if I have to."

"I think you need to eat."

"There's a Cheesecake Factory a few miles down the road, how does—"

"YES! You had me at cheesecake."

He laughed. "Great."

He drove to the restaurant, which was at a mall on the north side of the city. It was still a bit early for the dinner crowd, so we found a great parking space near the door.

Our luck continued inside, and the hostess seated us immediately. I loved the Cheesecake Factory, but I was well aware their portion sizes were huge and probably wouldn't leave much room for dessert. So, I ordered soup and cheesecake.

Orders placed, we sat in awkward silence for a few minutes. "Are we going to address the elephant in the room?"

I raised an eyebrow, puzzled. "Which one?"

"There's more than one?" He chuckled. "I'm talking about the murder."

I shrugged. "What's to talk about?"

"It's pretty clear you believe Dallas Simpson killed his wife." He looked at me. "Why?"

I took a few minutes to gather my thoughts. "I don't know. I guess because my first instinct when I saw the woman in the kennel area was that it was Keri Lynn. So, who else would want to murder her?"

"There's no other reason you can think of for why her husband might want her dead?"

"Honestly, I don't know either one of them. I only met them for the first time a few days ago."

"Tell me about it."

I told Red about the dog show and my meeting with Keri Lynn and later with Dallas. He asked a few questions but mostly let me talk.

The waiter brought our food, and we continued to talk while I ate my soup, which was more than enough and left room for my cheesecake. Red didn't fare as well. His meal was huge, and he only had room for a couple of bites of my cheesecake.

"So, you didn't like Dallas Simpson because he was tanned?" he asked.

I thought back and tried to remember my impressions from Saturday. "It wasn't just because he was *overly* tanned. It's because of his air of superiority. Plus, he seemed like one of those men who think they're God's gift to women and flirt with everyone in a skirt, regardless of age."

"You got all this based on a few minutes of talking to him about boarding your dog?"

"Pretty much." I scowled. "Well, for some reason, I got the impression maybe there was something going on between him and the girl who checked Aggie in at the resort, Heather."

He looked up. "You know her last name?"

I shook my head. "No, she just said Heather."

"What made you think there was something going on? Was he there?"

"Noooo." I shook my head and thought back. "I think it was because she kept slipping and calling him by his first name and then correcting herself. So she would say, Dallas…ah, I mean Mr. Simpson. If she had just called him Dallas, I probably wouldn't have thought twice about it. I didn't know him. I would have just thought that's how things were. Maybe everyone called him by his first name."

He nodded. "So, the fact she kept stopping herself and correcting it drew attention to the fact she shouldn't be using his first name." He smiled. "Very perceptive of you."

For some reason, receiving praise from him made me self-conscious and heat rose up my neck.

I paused for a moment. "When I first saw Keri Lynn at the dog show, there was a man in the tent with her."

"Her husband?"

I shook my head. "No, but I got the impression he and Keri Lynn were… close." I stared across the table. "If you get my drift."

He nodded. "Was it anything in particular you noticed?"

I thought back but shook my head. "Not really. It was more of a feeling than anything else." I shook my head. "I guess that wasn't very helpful."

He reached across and squeezed my hand. "It might be very helpful. At this stage, we need anything we can get. Maybe he and Keri Lynn were involved in an affair and she broke it off."

"And so he killed her?"

"Maybe." He squeezed my hand again. "Anything else?"

I thought for a minute and then shook my head. "Not really." I looked at him. "Now it's my turn."

He opened his hands and sat back. "Fire away."

"What happens now?"

"Tomorrow I'll see where we stand with the forensics team. I'll also check to see if Mrs. Simpson has returned from her dog show. I asked Officer Lewis to get all of the details and if necessary, we'll have the local police make a trip to the show and get a visual confirmation."

"How will they do that?"

"We have her driver's license picture. They'll confirm and take a picture of her and send it to me."

"You really did believe me," I said quietly. "I feel so ashamed for behaving like some lovesick teenager."

He reached over and gave my hand a squeeze. "Hey, we've moved on."

I nodded.

The waiter brought our bill and Red paid. As we were leaving, I noticed he had a smile on his face. "What?"

"Lovesick?"

I gave him a playful punch, and he laughed.

For the remainder of the car ride, we talked about possible reasons for the murder, and I went over what I'd seen on the pet cam for what felt like the millionth time.

I'd told him I'd left my car at the museum, so I was surprised when we got to Chattanooga that instead of taking Interstate 24, which would take him downtown to my car, he continued north on Interstate 75. "Where are you going?"

"Pet Haven. I'm not letting you go back to that place by yourself."

I was grateful it was now dark and he couldn't see my smile. Taking me to pick up Aggie meant going out of his way, but I was extremely grateful. I was struggling to forgive myself for doubting him previously. I'd have to think of a way to make it up to him.

When we arrived at Pet Haven, he pressed the button for the security gate and gave my name to the security guard, who opened the gate so we could enter. Inside, he drove to the main building. We got out of the car and walked to the door, where we waited for the security guard to unlock it for us. While we waited, I noticed Red looking at the security cameras. "This place has better security than some banks I've been to."

I followed his gaze and noticed the discreetly placed cameras affixed around the building for the first time.

Inside, I gave the security guard the papers proving Aggie was my dog. He asked for my driver's license, which he said was required to prove I was who I claimed to be and had the right to take her. Finally, convinced that I was indeed Aggie's owner and had the right to pay the astronomical fee, he processed my credit card and then went back to get her.

"Are you kidding? It cost more to board your dog than it cost to stay at the Ritz-Carlton hotel?"

I sighed. "I should have tucked her in my purse and taken her with me."

After a few minutes, the guard came back. He had Aggie on a leash, and she walked with her huge bone treat in her mouth and he carried a bag.

The guard handed me the leash and Red the bag, which I saw contained some of the stuffed toys I'd seen on her bed when I watched her on the pet cam. "Sorry, but she wouldn't let go of the bone. She growled whenever I tried to take it."

The bone was still large, but she'd managed to remove most of one end. I bent down to greet her. She growled when I tried to remove the bone too, but I wasn't giving in to a six-pound dog. With one snatch, I took it away and shoved it in the bag. She spun around for a bit but eventually gave in and leapt into my arms.

We hugged and cuddled, and she covered my face with kisses.

"Ahem." Red coughed.

"Oh, sorry." I turned and carried her out of the building.

I went to put her in the back of the car, but she had her paws in my sweater and refused to let go.

I made a few attempts to extract my sweater from her claws but realized there was no way I was going to be able to get her off without damaging my sweater. I thought for a second and realized I liked this sweater too much to ruin it to prove she wasn't the boss of me. It just wasn't worth the effort. So I gave up and got in the front seat. Aggie was stuck to my sweater like a large brooch. When I fastened my seat belt, she climbed onto my shoulder like a parrot.

Red started the car, and I noticed the corners of his mouth twitching. "How do you plan to get her off?"

"When I get home, I'll take the sweater off."

He chuckled. "Round one goes to Aggie."

"Shut up!"

Chapter 6

Red drove me back to the museum to get my car. By the time I got in my own car, Aggie must have felt she'd proved her point. She retracted her nails and voluntarily moved to the back seat. Red and I said our good-byes, and he promised to call the next day.

The drive back to the hotel was uneventful. Although, after two days at the Ritz-Carlton, I had to admit, my room felt shabby and outdated. I noticed the matted, threadbare spots on the carpet, the scuff marks and scratches on the furniture, and the faded curtains more than I had before.

I made myself a cup of tea and sat in bed. Aggie curled up next to me and rested her head on my leg. Her chest rose and fell, her eyelids drooped, and I felt at peace. I had been a wife and was the mother of two wonderful children whom I would sacrifice my life for. I had good friends, like Dixie, whom I'd known for years. I also had new friends like Red. I smiled at the thought of where that friendship could go. However, there was nothing that quite compared to the love of this little six-pound dog. She loved me with her whole heart and had risked her life to protect me. When I unwittingly moved my leg, her eyes popped open, and she looked at me with love and adoration.

I picked her up and hugged her close. "I love you, Aggie."

Aggie gave my ear a lick and released a sigh that made me laugh.

"Okay, I'll let you sleep." I put her back down. She climbed on my lap and curled into a ball and then lay down.

I picked up my notepad from my nightstand and grabbed a pen. Using Aggie as a lap desk, I gently rested my notepad on her back.

She didn't seem to mind.

I was eager to get everything Red told me written down before I forgot something. So I jotted down everything I could remember from our conversation and made notes of questions as they popped into my head.

Why would Dallas Simpson want to kill his wife? Was Dallas having an affair with Heather? Even if he was having an affair with Heather, why would he need to kill his wife? Divorce wasn't taboo, as in previous centuries. If Dallas wanted a divorce, he could get one pretty easy. I knew, from personal experience, there were forms online, and for about fifty dollars, he could be divorced without much fuss, as long as there weren't young children included. "I wonder if they have children?" I made a note to find out. I continued to mutter to myself, "Owning a building would make splitting assets harder." I made another note to ask my daughter, Stephanie. One partner would most likely need to buy out the other person's equity in the business, which could be really messy. My experience from my days as a CPA had proven that rarely were two people equal when it came to a business. One person usually invested more money or time and felt they were entitled to more when it came time to split. I seriously doubted a married couple would think to draw up a partnership agreement. I made another note to find out if Pet Haven was a sole proprietorship, a limited liability partnership, or an S-corp.

I tapped my pen on the notepad. Aggie opened her eyes, but she was used to me talking to myself. She sighed, closed her eyes, and went back to sleep.

"There was no need to kill Keri Lynn. Unless…maybe he had a hefty life insurance policy on her." I scribbled down a note to try to find out. I had no idea how you found out things like that, but I was sure Red would know.

Both Dallas and Keri Lynn had an air of wealth about them. From Keri Lynn's manicured nails, perfectly colored hair, and designer clothes to Dallas's tan, which must have taken many hours in a tanning bed to achieve, his highlights, and expensive watch, there was an…aura of wealth and privilege. I could easily imagine them golfing in Scotland, sailing around the south of France, or going to the casinos of Monte Carlo. I knew without ever seeing it that Dallas would drive a luxury German car. I'd stake money he drove a BMW. He would live in a big fancy house. "There's one way to find out." I picked up my cell phone from the nightstand and did a quick search. A street name in a nearby Georgia town right across the border from Tennessee popped up for Keri Lynn and Dallas Simpson. The listing gave the street name but not the address, but from my house hunting excursions with Monica Jill, I recognized the street. It was in an exclusive gated golf course community with luxury homes that straddled the Tennessee and Georgia state lines. Houses in that subdivision were massive and came with massive price tags.

Money seemed to be the most logical reason to me. I couldn't imagine Dallas was jealous, although I supposed it was possible. I remembered seeing Keri Lynn with the man in the tent. Could they have been having an affair? What if he was a jilted lover? Could the man in the tent have killed her? I made a few notes to check if Red was able to find out who he was. Maybe jealousy was the motive. I mulled both ideas around for a moment and then moved back to Dallas. He seemed like the type of person who would need a lot of money. Pet Haven seemed to be very successful. The facility was vast. They had certainly invested a great deal of money into the gated entry, intercom system, marble-floored lobby, pet cams, televisions, masseuse, chefs, and everything else. Maybe Pet Haven was in trouble financially. I made a note to check into their finances. As a CPA, I knew looks could be deceptive. Just because Pet Haven seemed to be successful, it was possible the business could be in debt up to its eyeballs. Pet Haven charged exorbitant fees for their services, but in all honesty, I couldn't fault them for that. I moved my notepad and watched Aggie sleep. As a relatively new pet owner, I loved my dog and treated her like a member of my family. I wanted the best for her, and Pet Haven certainly seemed to offer the best. Dallas and Keri Lynn had identified a gap and were filling a need. Nevertheless, I spent a few minutes thinking of ways to find out about their financial situation. They were a private company, so their records wouldn't be easily accessible, like a publicly traded company. However, there were ways. In fact, a crazy idea crossed my mind. I tapped my pen on my notepad. It was a very crazy idea, and Red would absolutely hate it, but there wasn't really anything he could do to stop me. I rolled the idea around in my brain.

"Maybe I should marinate on this a bit longer." I turned out the lamp and slid down under the covers. However, in my heart, I knew I'd already made up my mind. I just needed to figure out a way to make it work.

Chapter 7

Tuesday morning, I went through my normal routine. I dressed, took care of Aggie, and drove to work, despite the fact Linda Kay had sent a text letting me know I didn't need to go in to work that day. Jacob was out with a broken ankle, and she and Edward were taking their time driving back to Chattanooga. They were going to take the back roads rather than the interstate so they could stop at a few antique shops along the way. However, I had a few things I wanted to get cleaned up, so I went to work as usual.

I spent the morning tying up loose ends with the end-of-the-month accounting and preparation for filing taxes. Most people didn't realize nonprofit organizations still had to file tax returns every year, but they did. Nonprofits must file a return, but if they're recognized as 501C3s, they wouldn't have to pay taxes. It was early for thinking about taxes, which wouldn't be filed until May, five months from now. However, as a temporary employee, I wasn't sure how long I'd be working for the museum. My assignment wasn't firm. The museum could decide my services were no longer needed tomorrow, and that would be the end of my job security. I doubted if Linda Kay would let that happen. I knew she was fighting to get a permanent position added, but I also knew the decision was outside of her control. Regardless of whether I was still working in May or not, I wanted everything to be ready for whoever filed the forms.

I planned to leave at noon, but right before I was getting ready to go, I got a call from my bank.

I'd forwarded the sales contract for the house to the mortgage broker I'd been working with right after Monica Jill sent it to me.

"Hello, Denise," I said cheerfully.

After the first few moments, my smile was gone from my face and my voice. "What do you mean you might not be able to approve my loan? You already approved it. I got preapproved before I started house hunting."

I had never met Denise, but her voice sounded young. She told me there had been a change in my credit ranking from the time she initially preapproved me for the loan and now. She said my credit was fine, but apparently my husband had a lot of debt, which was impacting my credit score. He'd maxed out his credit card and purchased a condo and a new car.

"My husband? Albert? How on earth is Albert buying a condo or using credit cards? He's dead."

Denise rattled off a Social Security number, which I verified was indeed my late husband's. "Then it looks like your husband is the victim of identity theft."

"But I have a death certificate. How is anyone getting credit when he's dead?"

Denise was sympathetic and promised to talk to her supervisor to find out what, if anything, they could do to help me. However, it was up to me to get busy working with the credit bureaus to make sure nothing would be connected to me in any way. Given the fact Albert was dead, this should be easy, but someone had managed to get credit for a dead person, and companies who had been fleeced were often anxious to locate anyone they could to help collect either their property or their money.

When I hung up, I sat for several minutes and stared out the window at the Tennessee River without really seeing it. When I finally shook myself, I grabbed my cell phone and quickly dialed my daughter.

"Stephanie?"

"Hi, Mom. How's Atlanta?"

I explained that I was back in Chattanooga and quickly shared the reason for my call.

She listened patiently while I explained what I'd just learned from the bank. She asked a few questions. I gave her both my Social Security number and that of her father, although I knew, as a lawyer, she had access to the information. I wanted to make it as easy as possible for her.

"That's despicable. It's like Dad's been victimized twice. First someone murders him, and now they murder his name by destroying his credit."

"I know, dear. I can try to take care of this, but—"

"I'm fine. In fact, I'd love to fight this battle. This makes me so angry."

All of her life, Stephanie had been a protector of the innocent. It was the reason she chose law. Even though she worked for a big firm in Chicago, she handled a lot of pro bono work and loved cases that involved the little guy who was being bullied by the system or large corporations.

"Thank you. How's Lucky? Oh, and Joe?"

Stephanie laughed. "I love how you ask about my dog before you ask about my boyfriend." She chuckled. "Both are doing well. Lucky is actually lying in a dog bed under my desk even as we speak."

"Your job lets you bring your dog to work?"

"He's so well-behaved, and with the training he's had, everyone loves him. When people are stressed, they come in and play with him and it helps them feel better. Plus, Joe got him certified as a registered therapy dog like Aunt Dixie recommended."

I smiled at the way my children took to Dixie and referred to her as their aunt, even though there was no blood relationship between us. "Joe did it?"

"Well, I could have taken him, but he was so much more familiar with the rules for the test."

I hoped one day to get Aggie tested to be a registered therapy dog. Dixie's dogs were registered therapy dogs, and she had told us about Therapy Dogs International, which performed the tests to ensure a dog had the proper temperament to go into nursing homes and hospitals. There were studies that showed people recovered better when they had a dog to pet. However, I'd briefly looked at the requirements for the testing. It wasn't anything difficult, but a few of the exercises would be a challenge, like greeting a friendly stranger without pouncing on them and not being skittish around wheelchairs, walkers, or crutches. The hardest for Aggie would be leaving food that had dropped on the floor. In fact, I asked Dixie why that was even important. She mentioned how at nursing homes and hospitals she had occasionally encountered pills on the floor and that it was important that a dog was trained not to quickly eat something dropped.

"So Lucky is a registered therapy dog now?"

I could hear the pride in her voice. "Yes, and, Mom, it's been amazing. I had a case involving a little kid who rarely speaks to anyone except her brother. I needed to question her and I brought Lucky. She just sat on the floor and petted him. She talked to Lucky and answered every one of my questions."

"That's great, honey."

We talked for a few moments and then hung up with promises to speak over the weekend.

I sat for a few minutes and thought about the series of events that led to both my daughter's and my own happiness. We met Officer Joe Harrison when he came by to notify us that my husband, Albert, was dead. Joe was on the K-9 division for the Lighthouse Dunes Police Department. There was an instant connection between him and Stephanie. When I moved to Chattanooga and Aggie found a dead body while Joe and Stephanie were visiting, it was Joe who called an old friend from his military days, Red Olson, who was with the TBI, to look after us when he had to return to Indiana. I wouldn't say there was an instant connection between Red and me, but we were finding our way.

I said a brief prayer of thanks and once again, prepared to leave. This time when my phone rang, it was Dixie.

"Aren't you supposed to be enjoying your anniversary?"

Dixie laughed. "Hello to you too."

"I'm sorry. Hello, and how are you and Beau?"

"We're fine, but the anniversary trip to Gatlinburg will have to be rescheduled."

"What happened?"

"Are you free for a late lunch? I'm downtown."

"I'm starving."

We agreed to meet at a downtown tearoom I loved. I grabbed my purse, and this time I made it out of the museum without interruption.

The English Tea House was a quaint shop near the Chattanooga Choo Choo that not only served real British tea but also had a small gift shop where you could buy clotted cream, teacups, and hard-to-find British food items like Marmite, frozen faggot, and spotted dick. They even had real suet for those diehard expats interested in making their own spotted dick pudding.

Dixie had already arrived by the time I got there, and thankfully, she'd ordered the cream tea.

As soon as I sat down, I grabbed a scone, slathered strawberry preserves and clotted cream over it, and took a bite. It was delicious. There were sandwiches, pastries, and an extra plate of scones because, as Dixie liked to say, "This isn't our first rodeo." She loved scones as much as I did, and we'd both eaten our weight in them.

Once I'd eaten enough to take the edge off my hunger, I asked, "Why aren't you in Gatlinburg?"

Dixie explained that the storm that had passed through the other night had apparently taken out the power to the cabin she and her husband had reserved.

"It's an anniversary trip," I joked. "It's supposed to be romantic. You could have made a fire in the fireplace and snuggled together."

Dixie snorted. "I was not about to stay in the mountains with no lights, no heat, no hot water, no curling iron, no charge for my cell phone, and no food."

"The pictures you showed me of the cabin had a huge kitchen." In fact, the cabin was the most luxurious log cabin I'd ever seen. It included a hot tub and sauna, although, with no power, they wouldn't have been able to use those.

"What good is a kitchen when you can't put the food in the refrigerator and keep it cold? I wasn't about to put it outside so we could attract bears. Plus, the stove was electric. So…I made Beau pack up and take me home."

"Poor Beau."

She shook her head. "I wasn't that excited about being in the mountains anyway." She sipped her tea. "Now, what's going on with you?"

I had refrained from telling Dixie about the murder I'd witnessed, not wanting to ruin her anniversary, but now I filled her in on all of the details.

She listened in rapt silence. Her face reflected her shock at each major turn of events in the story. When I finally finished, she stared for several long moments.

"Wow! That's horrible to actually witness someone being brutally murdered." She shivered. "Are you okay?"

Dixie was one of the only people who had recognized how stressful it was for me to actually witness another human being killed. Her thoughtfulness and compassion brought a tear to my eye, but I quickly choked back the emotion.

"It was tough." I took a deep breath. "But I'm better now." I smiled at my friend to show her I really was working on getting that horrible memory out of my mind.

She smiled coyly. "Sounds like you and Red are doing well."

Heat rushed up my neck, and I quickly took a sip of tea to hide the smile forming on my lips. "We're fine—now." I stared into my cup to avoid the condemnation I deserved reflected in her eyes. "I'm ashamed at how I behaved." I shook my head. "I can't believe I hung up on him and acted like a teenager." I looked up. "I'm old enough to know that communication is vital in any relationship, yet when I thought he didn't trust me, the first thing I did was hang up and avoid talking."

I was surprised and pleased when Dixie reached out and squeezed my hand. I took a deep breath and got up the courage to look at her. I was thankful when, instead of disapproval, I saw compassion.

"Stop being so hard on yourself. No one's perfect, especially when the heart is involved. You've been through a lot of emotions in a short period of time with Albert's cheating on you with that stripper, his murder, moving six hundred miles away, then Aggie found that dead body, and being held hostage." She shook her head. "Frankly, I think you're doing pretty well, all things considered." She gave my hand another squeeze. "I'm just glad Red didn't give up." She smiled.

"So am I." I smiled back.

"Now what are you going to do?"

I was a bit puzzled. "Well, we went to dinner last night and we'll—"

"I mean about the murder."

I considered whether or not to share the crazy plan that I formulated last night.

"Spill it."

I pulled out my notebook. "I've been thinking about possible motives for why Dallas might kill his wife, and money seems the most logical thing to me."

She shrugged. "Agreed. Money can be a very powerful reason for murder, but how to prove it?"

"I was thinking we need someone on the inside."

She stopped her cup midway to her mouth. "What do you mean?"

"Well, I was thinking about seeing if he needed anyone to do his books."

"Are you crazy?" She put her cup down so quickly she spilled tea on the table. "You are deliberately going to work for someone you believe murdered his wife?" She stared at me as though I'd lost my mind.

"I don't think he knows I'm the one who reported seeing it, but I'll need to check with Red."

"Red is going to explode when he hears this." She narrowed her eyes. "You haven't told him yet, have you?"

I slowly shook my head.

"I want to be a fly on the wall for that one."

"Thanks... I was hoping you would help me." I couldn't hide the disappointment in my voice. Dixie had been there through the last few difficulties, and I relied on her wisdom and support. The fact that she always packed a gun was also helpful when dealing with murderers.

She sighed. "Of course I'll help you. You don't think I'm going to stand by while you single-handedly trap a murderer, do you?"

I smiled.

"Now, what's the plan?"

Chapter 8

Tuesday night meant obedience training. After lunch, I went back to my hotel room and spent a few hours of quality time with Aggie before driving to obedience class.

There were four people in the class. Monica Jill and her dog, Jac, were already in the building. I spent a few minutes and told her about the disappointing news from my bank.

"Honey, I'm so sorry." She hugged me. "But we're just going to pray and believe that God will make a way for you to get that house."

"Well, thank you." I smiled and turned to walk away.

"Where're you going?"

"I'm going to get ready for class." Unless she'd had a stroke in the last five seconds, she had to realize why we were here.

"Oh no, you don't, sister." She grabbed my hands, closed her eyes, and proceeded to pray for God to show favor for me with the bank and help me get approved for my mortgage.

I was still adapting to the Southern Bible Belt with bold Christians, where store clerks and waitresses ended conversations with "Have a blessed day" and where perfect strangers hugged and openly prayed for me in public forums. As a Catholic from Indiana, I wasn't ashamed of my faith, but I was also not as comfortable with public demonstrations.

Thankfully, her prayer was brief. When she finished, she hugged me. Unfortunately, we still had our dogs, and Jac and Aggie decided they were too close for comfort. As the dogs pulled away, our leashes got tangled and we were roped together like cattle. We had to cling to each other to avoid falling.

"Jac!" Monica Jill snapped her fingers. "Sit."

Obviously, she must have been practicing, because he quickly put his butt on the ground and looked up, expecting his treat.

It was easier for me to simply scoop Aggie up in my arms and unclip her leash.

We untangled our dogs just as the other members of the class arrived.

B.J. Thompson and her West Highland terrier, Snowball, waited by the bleachers. The last member of the class was Dr. Morgan and his German shepherd, Max. Dr. Morgan was a coroner. He was blunt, and when I first met him, I didn't like him. However, after he saved my life, I softened my opinion of him. Once I got to know him, I realized he was shy and socially awkward, which was probably why he chose to work with dead people. He wouldn't have to talk to his patients.

Dixie entered with Leia and Chyna, who regally walked into the building without pulling on their leashes. In fact, most times Dixie didn't even bother attaching their leashes, they were so well behaved. However, she believed in setting a good example, so she always used leashes at the dog club. They followed Dixie to the middle of the floor, where they stood, gazing at her face and waiting for a command before they lay down. Further amazing was the fact that they stayed there while she left the room to get her papers in the office, in spite of Snowball's barking and Jac's pulling on his leash as Monica Jill strained to keep him from running to the poodles. Even Max, the German shepherd, paced anxiously. Aggie considered the two standards part of her tribe and would have taken off for a quick round of catch me if you can if I wasn't still holding her. Even then, I had to tighten my hold to keep her from leaping out of my arms.

Dixie hurried back and started the class. Today's lesson involved learning to walk on a leash without pulling. She picked up the leash of one of the poodles and demonstrated the lesson, which, for her, involved walking with her dog on a loose leash. For us, our leashes were much shorter with less room for the dogs to get out of position. The exercise would involve starting with the dogs on our left sides in a sit. Treats in hand and in front of the dog's nose, we would give the command to heel and walk while the dog nibbled at the treat.

"Okay, now I want you all to try." Dixie gave a hand signal, which told her dog to return to her lounging position and watch the show.

"That's all good and fine for you people with big dogs, but how exactly am I supposed to do that?" B.J. said with her hand on her hip and a tilt to her head.

Dixie smiled. "It's not as easy with a small dog because you'll need to bend over more, which is why you and Lilly Ann should move to the back of the line."

B.J. was already at the back of our line, but I was second behind Dr. Morgan and Max. I stepped aside, and Monica Jill and I switched positions. I was now in third place.

"Now." Dixie took Snowball's leash. She wrapped the leash around her hand to remove the slack, leaving just enough for the dog to sit comfortably by her leg. She reached in the treat bag she always wore around her waist and pulled out a small piece of what I knew was dried liver. The foul-smelling treat had Snowball's ears standing up at attention and her eyes fixed on Dixie's hand. Dixie bent over so she had the treat at the dog's nose and then said, "Heel."

Dixie took a small step forward, and Snowball followed the treat like the Pied Piper. In that position, Dixie couldn't walk quickly, but she and Snowball went about six feet. When Dixie stopped, she said, "Sit." She positioned the treat so the dog's butt immediately went down, and the instant it touched the ground, she gave her the treat and praised the dog. "Good girl." She returned the leash to B.J.

"Traitor." B.J. stared at Snowball, who was too intent on licking up any crumbs that might have escaped and landed on the floor to care what her owner said.

"Okay, now let's all try it."

We spent almost the entire time working on heeling, stopping, and then heeling again. By the end of class, my back was sore from bending over, but I was pleased at Aggie's progress.

Dixie always left time at the end of class to answer any questions we had.

Dr. Morgan raised a hand. "Max does great here, but when we're at the park, he couldn't care less about listening, no matter what soul-selling treats I use."

Dixie made a point of instructing that we use really good treats when training our dogs. The treats needed to be good enough that our dogs would "sell their souls" to get them.

She nodded. "Honestly, that's normal because we've been practicing in an environment without distractions. It's going to be hard for your dogs, who are all pretty young, to choose training when there are other dogs' butts to sniff or squirrels to chase."

We chuckled.

"However, in a week or so, once we know the dogs fully understand what we want, then we'll make it harder by adding distractions. Eventually, your dog will understand what is expected and will be consistent, regardless of the environment."

I walked over to the bleachers where Monica Jill and B.J. were talking. "You still taking Jac to Pet Haven for doggie day care?" I asked.

"Yes. Dixie recommended it. It's been a lifesaver. He loves it." She looked lovingly at her dog, who was trying to get Snowball to play with him. Unfortunately, the Westie was more interested in getting Max's attention.

"When he comes home from day care, he's exhausted. Those are the only days I get rest from having to play ball with him."

He had a red ball in his mouth, and he was using every trick he knew to get Snowball's attention.

"I take Snowball to Pet Haven too." B.J. yanked on the small dog's leash to keep her from trying to hump the German shepherd. "Snowball, stop." She pulled the dog away and looked at us sheepishly. "The little floozy has absolutely no shame in her game."

We laughed.

"Speaking of floozies, I had to go out of town for work and I boarded Aggie at Pet Haven."

"Okay, what kind of work were you doing?" B.J. laughed.

Heat rose up my neck. "No, not me. I mean…I just felt like the owner, Dallas, well…he seemed a bit…well…"

B.J. laughed and gave me a playful shove. "Girl, I know what you mean. That Dallas is terrible. He'll flirt with anything in a skirt."

Monica Jill laughed. "B.J.'s right. He flirts with all the staff, the customers… everybody. I don't know why Keri Lynn puts up with it."

B.J. leaned close and whispered, "Well, I can guess why she puts up with it." She winked. "But I certainly wouldn't put up with it. If my husband flirted with women like Dallas does, I'd take my gun and shoot him." She laughed.

Monica Jill got serious. "I think Keri Lynn does her own fair share of flirting."

"What do you mean?" I asked.

"You saw that man in the tent with her at the dog show?"

I nodded.

"That's Justin, he's the chef at Pet Haven. He has the world's biggest crush on Keri Lynn."

"Does she like him too?" I frowned at the sound of my own voice, which reminded me of middle school.

Monica Jill looked down her nose at me in a way that said, *"Are you serious?"* "I think Keri Lynn likes men. She flirts and most of them know she isn't serious. I mean, the woman is absolutely gorgeous. However, someone like Justin…well, it's just cruel to flirt with someone like that."

"Like what?" I asked.

"Someone who's…simple, like Justin." She sighed. "He's naïve and extremely gullible. If he thought someone like Keri Lynn was interested in him, he'd fall all over himself to please her. I doubt there's anything he wouldn't do for her." She reached out her hand and hurried to explain. "I don't mean there's anything really wrong with him, but he's just…well, simple."

"Sounds like Keri Lynn is taking advantage," I said.

She shrugged. "Maybe, but we don't know for sure, and I like to give people the benefit of the doubt." She shrugged. "Seriously, I love Pet Haven." She looked at me. "How did Aggie like it?"

"She loved it." I struggled to figure out how to get the conversation back to Dallas.

Dixie joined the conversation. "He seems pretty sleazy to me. Do you think he's all talk?"

Monica Jill and B.J. both shrugged.

"Honey, no man could be as…in demand as Dallas Simpson thinks himself capable. I'm sure he's all talk and very little action." B.J. paused. "Although…"

"What?" I asked.

She shrugged. "I don't like to spread gossip, but I noticed one of those pretty young things he has working there seemed a bit…overly friendly, if you know what I mean." She looked pointedly at us, and we all nodded.

"Was it Heather?" I asked.

She shrugged. "Honey, most days, I'm doing good to remember my own name. I sure ain't trying to remember any names I don't have to."

"Blond, young…perky?" I tried again.

She shrugged. "I guess, but I can't say." She squinted and tilted her head. "Why you wanna know? Don't tell me you've got the hots for Dallas Simpson."

"No. No. No. Absolutely, no."

She folded her arms, gave a cynical smirk, and pursed her lips. "Uh-huh." I sighed and glanced at Dixie.

She gave a slight shrug and a barely perceptible nod.

"I think there's something weird going on at Pet Haven." I briefly told them about seeing someone murdered.

"Good lawd." B.J. rubbed her arms. "That made the hair on my arms stand up."

Monica Jill stood quietly.

I looked at her. "What do you think? I mean, we found her with a man in the tent in a compromising position, and he was definitely not her husband."

Her face turned red. "I don't think people should speculate about stuff like that. That's how rumors get started, and murder isn't anything to joke about." She grabbed her purse. "Maybe people should pray for them, rather than spreading rumors."

I was momentarily shocked by her response. "I'm not spreading—"

"Come on, Jac." She gave her leash a yank and stormed out of the building.

We stared after her for several seconds.

Finally, B.J. said, "I wonder what's got her panties in a wad."

"I have no idea." I stared from the door where she left to Dixie, who merely shook her head.

I had completely forgotten Dr. Morgan was still there until he spoke. "I think someone spread some pretty awful rumors about her husband about a year or so ago. He almost lost his job, and they went through a rough patch. So…"

I looked at him. "I'm sorry, but…"

He gave a curt laugh. "How do I know?"

"Well, yeah."

He sighed. "I work with her husband, Zach, at the county."

"I'm sorry. I had no idea."

He shrugged and then tipped his head toward us and walked out with Max.

"Honey, you didn't know. I'm sure she'll be as right as rain by tomorrow." B.J. gave me a quick hug. "I live in the same subdivision with the Simpsons, but we rarely see each other. Next time I drop Snowball off for day care, I'll pay better attention." She hurried out.

I waited while Dixie turned out the lights and made sure the office was locked up. When she returned to the gym area, she turned to face Leia and Chyna, who were still lying in the middle of the floor. "Free."

Both dogs stretched and slowly trotted to Dixie's side.

We all walked out together. Dixie locked the door.

Once outside, the poodles wandered to the side of the building, where they found a patch of grass. They squatted and took care of their business. Unlike the well-trained standards, Aggie couldn't be trusted off-leash. So I walked her over to the grass so she could join her friends. She sniffed until she found the perfect blade of grass and then squatted too.

Dixie opened the side of her RV, and the standards climbed inside. She closed the door and turned to face me. "Look, I'm sure Monica Jill will be okay. She's not the type to hold a grudge for long. She'll blow off steam, and then she'll be her perky, annoyingly optimistic self in no time."

"I hope so. I like her."

Dixie smiled. "I like her too."

I spent the entire drive back to the hotel beating myself up mentally for upsetting someone who had done so much for me. Not only had Monica Jill spent a great deal of time and money helping me find a house, but she had also been a friend to me. I thought about how just a short time earlier she'd prayed for me when she learned about the identity theft. I owed her an apology, and by the time I made it back to my room, I was determined I'd give her one.

At the hotel, I encouraged Aggie to take care of her business before we went inside, but she had other ideas. Instead of at least trying, she took the time to wander, bark at a passing squirrel, and play with a discarded paper cup. I gave up and we went inside.

I intended to immediately send an apology text to Monica Jill but got distracted when my phone rang. I looked at the picture that was displayed and smiled at the face of my son, David, even though he couldn't see me. "David, how are you?" I glanced at my watch. "I thought you were in Milan. What time is it there?"

"I was in Milan, but I'm back in New York."

David was a successful stage actor who was supposed to be on tour in Europe.

"Don't tell me the play closed?" From the clippings he'd sent and the information I'd found online, it looked as though the play was very well received.

"The play's doing well, but a pipe burst at the theater and everything's flooded. So it looks like we've got a little time off while they make repairs. I thought I'd come for a visit if you were up to it."

"Of course. I'd love to see you." I looked around the hotel room.

"Why do I feel a 'but' coming. It's okay if you've got plans. Stephanie told me about your...friend."

"Nothing like that. It's just that I moved out of the house I was renting and I'm in a hotel, but I'd love to see you."

We talked for several minutes and finalized the arrangements.

When I got off the phone, I was surprised when it rang again. This time it was Monica Jill. I took a deep breath before I answered. "Monica Jill.

I'm so glad you called. I wanted to apologize for earlier tonight. I didn't mean to be disrespectful or hurtful or start rumors. I was—"

"It's okay. I know you didn't mean any harm." She sighed. "I knew I overreacted the moment I pulled away, and I wanted to turn around and go back and apologize for getting in a huff, but I had some real estate stuff, and this is the first chance I got to call. I know your heart, and I know you weren't trying to cause problems."

"Thank you. I was just about to call and apologize to you."

She *tsk*ed. "No need. I'm fine. Hey, apart from apologizing, the reason I called was because one of the Realtors I talked to was the listing agent for your house."

I smiled at Monica Jill's energy and optimism. Based on the news from my bank, it was encouraging to see she still considered it "my house."

"I told him you might need an extension while you cleared up the identify theft situation with your late husband. And you'll never guess what he said."

I sat down on the bed and tried to brace myself. I couldn't imagine what he could possibly say. "What?"

"Well, he's real good friends with the owner. He said the house has been used as a rental, and he's pretty sure the owner will let you rent the house while you work on the mortgage."

I wasn't expecting that. "Really?" I tried to mentally process that bit of news. "How much would he want for rent? Does he know I have a dog?"

I nearly dropped the phone when she told me the rental price. It was well below what I'd paid for my last rental. In fact, it was less than I was paying for the hotel.

The excitement in her voice bubbled over. "Yes, I told him all about Aggie. I told him what a cute, well-behaved little dog she is."

"Why is the rent so cheap?" I couldn't help wondering what was wrong with the house that he was willing to rent it for so little.

"Well, the owner is a doctor. The house used to belong to his grandmother. He's been renting it for about two years since she had to go in a nursing home. So, he doesn't need the money."

"Everyone needs money."

"He's more interested in having someone in the house who'll take care of it. Plus, you'll have all of the utilities to pay. The insurance on an empty house is outrageous, and he doesn't want to be bothered with the yard or any of the upkeep." She hesitated. "Honestly, I thought you'd be excited."

"I am excited. I just…I guess, I'm in shock. I wasn't expecting it."

"Well, girlfriend, if you want to rent it, it's yours. You just say the word and I'll call him back."

I looked around and had a moment of panic when I didn't see Aggie. She had been unusually quiet while I was on the phone. I walked around the side of the bed and found she had pulled my remaining pillow from the bed. She had ripped open a seam and was covered in feathers. I sighed. "Deal!"

Chapter 9

Monica Jill worked quickly, and by the next day, I had signed a rental agreement and had keys to the house. The owner had my check for the first and last months' rent and a hefty pet deposit. Similar to my last move, Dixie turned on the Southern charm and worked her magic. My belongings were out of storage and transported to my soon-to-be new home.

Linda Kay was more than enthusiastic and told me to take as much time as I needed. By late afternoon, movers were hauling boxes and setting up beds and other large pieces of furniture. The house was organized chaos, and Dixie was the general. She gave orders and kept things moving.

Unlike my last move, I didn't have to worry about Aggie or confine her to a crate. The large fenced-in backyard allowed all three poodles to remain outside through the bedlam and confusion. While they chose to remain on the deck the majority of the time with their noses pressed up to the sliding glass door rather than running around the yard, it was still a better setup.

David's flight was scheduled to arrive at eight, so the guest bedroom and bathroom were the first things I set up. Monica Jill showed up with Jac late afternoon and brought food. The movers continued hauling boxes while we took a break to eat. The only flat surface that wasn't covered by boxes was the patio table, so the three of us went outside.

I hadn't realized how hungry I was until I smelled the spaghetti, salad, and garlic bread she brought, along with a gallon of sweet tea. Thinking of everything, she also brought paper plates, cups, and plastic silverware.

I expected to have to fight off Aggie and the other dogs, but the moment she let Jac out, a fierce game of chase ensued. Jac took off, with three poodles in hot pursuit.

We sat and watched the chase and ate.

"That dog wears me out." She watched Jac make a sharp turn and race around a tree. "We need a yard like this where he can run and play and get rid of some energy."

"He's just young," Dixie said.

"He's the same age as Aggie, and she's not wild."

Dixie chuckled. "Aggie is a different breed. Plus, she's a female. Males are often more...energetic."

"Well, he's certainly got plenty of energy."

We ate in silence for a bit. When we finished, Dixie brought out a large container of water for the dogs, which they lapped up eagerly.

Monica Jill packed away the leftovers and took them inside. When she returned, she called Jac, who rushed to her. She clipped his leash on. "He'll sleep like a log when he gets home." She smiled at her dog. "Tomorrow, we'll go to Pet Haven." She hesitated a moment and then turned to me. "I still think you're barking up the wrong tree. I think Dallas is like one of those fancy show ponies. He's playing the part of a gigolo. I think he worships his wife." She shook her head. "I think it's Keri Lynn who's been unfaithful. I saw her with that chef, Justin, and they weren't playing patty-cake."

"When?" I asked.

"Actually, last week when I went to pick him up from day care. He was so excited to see me, he piddled on the floor. I went in search of something to clean up."

"They made you clean it up?" I asked.

"No, but I wasn't going to leave it for someone else to clean." Monica Jill looked down her nose at me, but I merely shrugged.

Monica Jill continued, "When I walked by the employee break room, the door wasn't closed. I thought I'd just pop in and get some paper towels. That's when I saw them."

"What were they doing?" I asked.

She smirked with a you-must-be-joking look.

"What happened?"

"They didn't see me. I just closed the door and found the washroom." She sighed. "My husband's cousin is one of the groomers. I'll ask her if she's noticed anything...unusual."

"Be careful. I wouldn't want—"

She waved away my protest. "I'll be careful not to say too much." She looked down. "I'll be honest. I think you're wrong. I hope you're wrong." She sighed. "Even if you're right and he and Heather were cheating, it doesn't mean he killed his wife. It just means he's a low-down scumbag who doesn't honor his marriage vows and cheats on his wife. That doesn't make him a murderer."

"Agreed, but I know what I saw."

"But you said you couldn't see the person's face. It could have been someone else."

I thought for a moment. "It could have been."

"But it wasn't." She sighed.

I shrugged. "I'm pretty sure it was him."

She nodded.

We said our good-byes and I thanked her for the food and for helping me get out of the hotel and into a house, and then she left.

Red came by after work and helped unpack and move furniture. While he was placing the fancy dishes I rarely used at the top of the cabinets, he told me the latest news related to the case. "Forensics didn't find much. The area had been cleaned with bleach and cleaned well."

"Probably so he could hide evidence." I handed him the silver serving dishes I'd only used once in my entire married life.

"Or maybe they used bleach to sanitize the area." He put the silver at the back of the top shelf. "You're never going to be able to reach this stuff. Are you sure you want to put it in here?"

"I should just give it to Goodwill. I never use it, and it will be one less thing I need to clean." I sighed. "Although part of me wanted to hand it down to Stephanie when she gets married."

He chuckled. "I don't know your daughter well, but she doesn't strike me as the type to use this kind of silver service."

"You're right." I held out my hands and he took the silver items down and handed them back. I returned them to the box. "I'll donate it to Goodwill."

"Are you sure? This stuff is heavy. If it's real, it might be worth some money. Maybe you should sell it."

"Pshaw. Albert's mom gave it to us. Given how she felt about me, I doubt very seriously she spent a wad of money on it." I found the packing tape and secured the box. "Besides, this house doesn't have much storage. I will need to downsize. Any word from the police from the dog show?"

He shook his head. "Funny, she was supposed to be at the show for three days, but apparently, she packed up her tent and cleared out in the middle of the night."

I nearly dropped a glass and had to juggle to catch it. "Well, that's suspicious, don't you think? Before the police can get a good look at her, she scurries out in the middle of the night."

Infuriatingly, he merely shrugged. "She didn't know the police were coming."

"Oh yeah." I sighed.

"I asked her husband about her, and he promised he would have her call."

"Did she?"

He hesitated for several moments. "Not exactly. I got a text video." He pulled out his cell phone and made a few swipes. Then he held the phone so I could watch.

A tall, thin woman wearing a baseball cap, no makeup, and sunglasses, who looked a lot like Keri Lynn Simpson, appeared in the video. "Hello, Mr. Olson. This is Keri Lynn. My husband told me what's been going on. I want to assure you that I'm alive and well. I have a family emergency, and so I'm going to be hard to reach for a few days." She spun around and showed a rural area with plenty of trees. "As you can see, I'm off the beaten path and the cell reception isn't great. I should be back in a few days. I'll stop by as soon as..." The rest of her message was garbled and completely unintelligible.

"Were you able to trace it?" I looked at him.

He shook his head. "No, and we can't really tell where she is. We tried to get her cell phone carrier to help, but they couldn't even tell us which tower it pinged."

"Why not?"

He frowned. "Apparently, she wasn't using her cell phone."

I opened my mouth, but he held up a hand. "Before you ask, we checked with her husband. He said she dropped her phone and cracked the screen and she bought a cheap one at Walmart to use until she gets home and can get her phone repaired."

"That video wasn't very clear, and it could have been anyone."

"Maybe not anyone, but it looks like the photo we have of Keri Lynn."

I sighed. For the first time in two days, I questioned what I saw. Red's arm's encircled me.

He held me tightly and whispered, "I still believe you saw someone murdered. Maybe it wasn't Keri Lynn."

I sighed and put my head on his shoulder.

He leaned down to kiss me but suddenly stopped. He jerked his head up so suddenly, I stumbled.

"What?"

"Is that a gas stove?"

Since there were so many boxes in the kitchen, apparently he hadn't been able to see the stove until I moved the last box. Red loved to cook.

When I saw the excitement on his face, I couldn't be offended, but I teased him anyway. "I can't believe I've been replaced in your affections by a gas stove."

He pulled his eyes away from the stove and only then did he seem to realize what he'd done. "I'm so sorry. I just wasn't expecting that. Natural gas stoves are rare in Chattanooga." He grinned and then leaned down again, but this time it was Dixie who ruined the moment.

"Lilly Ann, you've got a million pillows. Are you sure you want—" Dixie came into the kitchen but halted. "Sorry." She turned around to leave.

We pulled apart.

"Wait. It's okay."

She turned around. "I didn't mean to interrupt."

Red looked at his watch. "I've got to go. I've got a presentation tomorrow, and I haven't even started."

I felt guilty. I knew Red was investigating Keri Lynn Simpson because of me when he probably should have been working on his other cases.

He kissed me and promised to call later and then hurried out the door.

Dixie stood in the kitchen holding four feather pillows. "You okay?"

I nodded. "He's investigating Keri Lynn and Dallas because of me. What if I'm wrong?"

"Are you?"

I shrugged. "I don't know anymore." I told Dixie about Keri Lynn's video. "I don't want Red to get in trouble."

"Red Olson is a grown man. He knows what he's doing. If he didn't want to investigate this, he wouldn't." She stared at me. "You've been confident about what you saw. I think you should trust yourself."

I nodded. "Thanks."

We worked a little longer, and then Dixie said she needed to get home. She loaded up the poodles and headed out to make her way up Lookout Mountain.

David's plane was scheduled to land soon. So I scooped up Aggie and headed for the Chattanooga airport.

Thankfully, Chattanooga's airport was small and traffic was light. Aggie and I pulled up to the curb just as I got a text message saying he had landed and would be out soon.

In just a few short minutes, David came out with a large backpack. He was wearing a baseball cap. I got out of the car and gave him a big hug. I opened the back hatch of my SUV and he tossed his backpack inside.

"Is that all the luggage you brought?"

He smiled. "When you travel as much as I do, you learn to pack light."

Aggie stood on her hind legs and put her nose to the crack I'd left in the back window. When she saw David, she immediately growled.

David quickly took off his baseball hat. "I forgot." He ran his hand over his head of short, curly dark hair and smiled at Aggie. She sniffed several times, and then her tail began to wag a hundred miles an hour, like a propeller.

He laughed. "Still afraid of men in caps?"

I nodded. From the corner of my eye, I saw the blue-shirted airport security guy heading toward us to hurry us along. We quickly got into the car and drove off.

On the way home, I told David about the house I planned to buy.

I pulled into the driveway.

"Why aren't you parking in the garage?"

"No garage door opener. The owner said he doesn't have one."

"You can get one of those universal remotes and I'll program it for you."

"Thanks."

We walked inside.

"I'm sorry about the boxes, but..."

He smiled and walked around, noticing all of the unique details. "I like the asymmetrical window and vaulted ceiling in your living room."

It was dark out now, so he wasn't able to see the wonderful backyard in all of its glory, but he seemed to appreciate it all the same.

I gave him a few minutes to get settled into the guest room.

The smell of spaghetti and garlic bread heating up in the oven drew him to the kitchen.

"Mmmm, that smells wonderful. When did you have time to cook?"

I laughed. "I didn't." I held up the bag from a chain restaurant.

Thanks to Dixie's handiwork, we were able to sit at the dining room table together. She had not only put away all of the items that had sat atop the table but had found my dishes and set the table as though company was coming.

Aggie wandered from David to me in the hopes of a handout or that one of us would drop something. It wasn't until all hope was lost that she gave up, went into the kitchen, and ate her dinner.

While we ate, I told David about the murder I'd witnessed.

He stared openmouthed at me. "That's absolutely horrible."

I also shared my plan to offer my services as an accountant so I could get a look at their books.

He was quiet, which I interpreted as judgment. Normally, David was supportive and slow to judge others, especially when it came to me. I had supported his dream to pursue a career as an actor, in spite of his father's opposition. So I was hurt but tried to hide it.

"I know you may not agree with my plan, but I feel strongly that someone should do something. Honestly, that's the problem with the world. No one wants to get involved."

He held up a hand. "Mom, calm down. I'm not opposed to your idea."

"You're not?"

He shook his head. "I was just thinking how I could get in on the action." He smiled. "Do you think they could use an actor on sabbatical or a volunteer dog walker?"

Chapter 10

David and I stayed up late figuring out a good cover story for him. We decided a place with that many dogs could always use a volunteer. In fact, he decided to play it as wanting to observe for a movie role. I felt that would appeal to Dallas's ego. This would give him a reason to hang out when I was at the museum.

Linda Kay had been so flexible and offered several times to allow me to work from home. I decided to take her up on the offer and would work half days at the museum and half days at Pet Haven. I could do this for at least a week. Hopefully, I could find out the financial health of Pet Haven by then.

After lunch, I drove home and picked up David and Aggie, and we headed to Pet Haven. Last night we'd agreed taking Aggie might make it harder for them to refuse. After all, if I was willing to pay their exorbitant fees for day care for my dog, and my son was willing to volunteer, then surely they couldn't object to free use of a certified public accountant.

I was grateful I'd made an appointment, because when I got to the security gate, the guard heard my name and immediately opened the gate so we could enter.

David whistled when he saw the marble lobby. "This is pretty spiffy for dogs." He looked around. "Maybe I should see if they could put me up too."

When we got to the front desk, there was a young woman I didn't recognize. "Mr. Simpson will be right out to meet you, Mrs. Echosby." She smiled.

Her name tag said her name was Madison. She smiled at me as she walked around the counter. She bent down to pet Aggie. "You're so cute."

Aggie's tail immediately wagged super fast.

When Madison reached in her pocket and pulled out a treat, the tail wagged even faster. "You're such a smart girl. I'll bet you know how to sit."

Aggie's butt hit the ground so fast I was shocked.

Madison smiled and promptly gave her the treat.

David leaned close and whispered, "Maybe you should get your friend to analyze those treats. I think they must be laced with something."

I glared, but he merely ignored me and bent down. "You certainly have a way with dogs." He smiled and turned up the charm.

Madison continued to pet Aggie. "I love dogs. That's why I wanted to work here."

"Me too." He extended a hand. "I'm David."

She shook. "Madison."

Dallas Simpson walked around the counter. "Mrs. Echosby." He smiled. I had expected a cold reception and had braced myself to grovel as I asked for forgiveness. However, I was shocked by the warm reception.

"Mr. Simpson. I'm so glad you—"

"Dallas, please." He grasped my hand in both of his. He then did what I thought impossible and smiled even bigger than before.

I fought the urge to extract my hand and turned to David. "This is my son, David."

He nodded to David and kept my hand clasped in his.

I was grateful when David extended a hand, forcing him to release me to shake.

He then bent over. "This lovely creature must be Aggie." He opened his arms, and my little traitor leapt up into his arms and began licking his face with a vengeance.

Dallas Simpson laughed and struggled to keep her from sticking her tongue in his mouth.

I was so surprised at her behavior, I was paralyzed.

David reacted faster and reached out and pulled Aggie off.

It wasn't until Aggie was removed that I noticed what she'd been up to. Dallas Simpson must have recently been refreshing his spray-on tan, which hadn't quite set. Aggie had managed to lick off a good portion from his face.

I gave credit to David for maintaining his composure because I was tempted to burst into laughter.

He turned to Madison. "Perhaps you wouldn't mind taking Aggie out to play with the small dogs while we chat."

Madison nodded and David handed Aggie over.

Dallas Simpson then turned back to us. "Why don't we go into my office and talk?" He extended an arm in the direction of the room he had just left.

We walked to the office and waited while he opened the door.

The office was large and plush. It contained the same marble flooring from the entry and a large plate-glass window that looked out on the back of the property. There was a white fuzzy rug under a glass desk and two clear plastic contemporary guest chairs.

David and I each sat in one of the chairs. The chairs were stylish, undoubtedly an interior designer's decision chosen purely for artistic merit rather than comfort. The plastic was hard and slippery, and I had to plant my feet on the rug and put both hands on the arms of the chairs to keep from sliding.

Unlike the hard plastic chairs provided for guests, Dallas Simpson had a large white desk chair that looked soft and comfortable. He gracefully sat down and leaned across the table. "Now, what can I do for you both?"

"First, I want to apologize for any inconvenience. I was genuinely concerned about your wife, Keri Lynn. However, it's obvious that my concerns were unfounded, and I wanted to apologize."

After I'd told David my impressions of Dallas Simpson's personality, he'd suggested a dramatic flowery apology would play best to his ego. If the gushing response Dallas Simpson provided was any indication, David had been right.

"My dear lady, think nothing of it." He waved his hand as though flinging away a gnat. "I'll admit it was a bit of an inconvenience, being taken down to the police station and questioned like a common criminal." He shuddered. "Those policemen probe into every aspect of your life." He pursed his lips. "I felt absolutely violated." He took two long, slow breaths. "However, I'm over it now." He leaned across the long, narrow desk, reached his hands out to me, and took one of mine that I'd failed to keep out of reach. "I harbor no ill feelings toward you. I believe your intentions were good, but I assure you, I love my wife."

"Thank you so much. I was so worried." I wrenched my hand away, reached in my purse, and took out a tissue to dab at my eyes, another suggestion of David's. He said if I felt myself about to burst out laughing, I should either pinch myself, bite the inside of my cheek, or get a tissue and feign tears.

"Honestly, Keri Lynn and I both laughed about it, but we were in no way offended. Please, don't distress yourself."

"I'm so thankful to you both." I dabbed the fake tears again and bit the inside of my jaw too for safe measure. "I'd like to apologize to Keri Lynn too…when she returns."

He shook his head. "I assure you. It isn't needed, but I will tell her."

"When do you expect her back?"

A muscle on the side of his face twitched, and his smile grew just the slightest bit colder. "I really couldn't say. She's dealing with a family emergency and...you know how these things are." He broadened his grin. At that moment, I knew what Red Riding Hood saw when she said, "Grandmother, what big teeth you have."

"I was hoping I could do something to make amends."

He opened his mouth to dismiss me, but I continued to speak. "I'm a CPA, and I know there's always a lot of work to finish off the fiscal year and get ready for filing taxes. I wondered if you would accept my offer to volunteer my services."

"You want to volunteer to do our taxes?"

I nodded. "Sure. It's the least I can do for the inconvenience I caused you." I hesitated. "That is, unless you already have a CPA to do them. I wouldn't want to step on anyone's toes."

"Well, honestly, Keri Lynn and I do the books ourselves. However, with my wife away tending to her family, it would be nice to have some help with all of that financial mumbo jumbo."

"I'd be more than happy to help."

"Are you sure? We could pay you."

I waved off the notion. "I wouldn't dream of it." I smiled. "I'm glad that's settled."

"Well, thank you." He smiled. This time it wasn't the scary wolf smile but the closest thing to sincerity I'd seen in him since we first met.

"I'd like to volunteer too." David leaned forward.

"Excuse me." I turned to David. "My son, David, is a very successful theatrical actor."

"Really?" He gave the *"you can't be very good, and you must be waiting tables"* look that I'd grown accustomed to whenever I told someone my son was an actor. "Would I have seen anything you were in?"

David rattled off a string of television shows and Tony Award–winning musicals he had performed in, and the look changed from skepticism to awe. "Wow. That's amazing. You know, Keri Lynn used to be an actress too." He smiled.

"Really? Theater? Film? Television?" David eagerly asked.

Dallas chuckled. "She did some modeling and made a few films, but well...things didn't work out quite as well for her acting career. She performed in a few little local performances...community theater." He swiveled his chair around and picked up a picture of Keri Lynn from the back of his desk. He stared at it for several moments before handing it to

David. "She's a beautiful woman. All the leading men fell in love with her." He smiled.

"What happened?" I asked.

"Well, you know how it is. She was young and wanted to be a star, and some men promised they could make her rich and famous." He took the picture back and replaced it. "Unfortunately, things didn't work out quite as well for her."

"I'm really sorry." I racked my brain to come up with a way to keep him talking, but it wasn't necessary.

He shrugged. "That's how she met her first husband. He owned a few magazines and a production company. They met and fell in love, but he died suddenly, and his family wasn't really interested in producing films."

"*Producing films starring Keri Lynn*" was left unsaid, but the implication was there nonetheless.

"So what brings you to Chattanooga?" He turned his attention to David.

David explained he was on a brief hiatus while the plumbing was being repaired in Milan, and he'd decided to come home to visit for a couple of weeks. "But the main reason I'm here is that I was hoping you'd permit me to do a bit of shadowing."

"I don't understand."

David leaned forward and lowered his voice. "Well, it's all very confidential, but I've just been cast in a new television series. It's going to be a modern remake of the old *Lassie* shows. You know…Timmy's grown and living in New York. He still has his best friend, Lassie, who has to get him out of all kinds of scrapes."

I didn't think the story sounded at all feasible, but Dallas Simpson was nodding like he thought this was the best idea he'd ever heard.

"That sounds fascinating."

"It's going to be great. They've got a fantastic dog trainer, and the dog who's going to play Lassie is actually the great-great-great-grand-dog of the original."

Dallas stared from David to me. "That's amazing." He shook his head. "But I don't see how I can help."

"I was hoping you'd let me observe you and some of the other dog trainers and staff so I can learn how they interact with the dogs." He laughed. "It's obvious from the way Aggie responded to you, you have a way with dogs."

Dallas Simpson laughed. "Well, I haven't been working with dogs very long, only the past two years. Before that, I worked in security."

"You mean like trading securities?" I asked.

He laughed. "No. Not that type of security. I mean security, like alarm systems. That's why when we started this place, we wanted the top-of-the-line security for our building. I'll admit I'm a bit of a technology-gadget nerd." He smiled big. "We wanted only the best for our clients."

There was a brief knock, and then the door opened. "Dallas, we need to talk. I was just—" A small-framed man wearing a white jacket entered. He wore thick glasses and had a weak chin and a bald spot on the top of his head. When he saw Dallas Simpson wasn't alone, he turned red and stammered. "I'm sorry. I didn't...uh...I didn't realize."

I'd seen Dallas Simpson exhibit many emotions. However, rage wasn't one until now. However, the look that flashed in his eyes was definitely not the happy-go-lucky ladies' man persona he'd adopted previously. "What do you want, Justin?"

Justin stormed over to the desk. "What's the meaning of this?" He slammed down a pink slip of paper on the desk, rattling the few items on top.

"It's a termination notice. Can't you read?" Dallas sneered.

"You can't fire me. Keri Lynn hired me. Only she can fire me." He glared.

"She's 'Mrs. Simpson' to you, and she's my wife." Dallas stood and glared at Justin. "We both own Pet Haven, and I can hire and fire whomever I want." His nostrils flared, and his eyes were mere slits.

Justin's chest rose and fell. His neck and face were beet red, and he looked as though he would explode at any second. He clenched his hands into fists, and I thought the two men would come to blows. However, as if flicking a switch, Justin's face suddenly relaxed, and he gave a snarky smile. He tugged at the sleeves of his shirt, revealing a gold watch. I was certainly no expert, but I'd say it was an expensive Rolex, similar to the one worn by Dallas.

At the sight of the watch, Dallas Simpson's face lost some of its color, and I would swear his eyes flashed with surprise. However, the emotion quickly vanished. "We'll just see who's fired when Keri Lynn returns." He turned and stomped out of the room.

Dallas took a deep breath and sat down. "I'm sorry about that. Keri Lynn felt sorry for the man and hired him, but he's gotten a bit too big for his britches." He took a few more deep breaths and forced a smile. "Where were we? Yes, you want to shadow me because I'm good with dogs." He turned to David.

"You definitely have a way with dogs, and it shows. I wouldn't just be observing. I want to help. I need to spend time with some of the dogs, get to know them. Obviously, with my schedule, I can't have a dog in New York, and I don't spend nearly enough time with Aggie." He looked at me. "So I want to make the most of the time while I'm here and immerse myself in the environment."

Dallas Simpson stared for a few moments, but then burst out in a huge smile. "Well, of course. I think that would be great. When do you want to start?"

"Would tomorrow be too soon?" David stood and extended his hand.

* * * *

David and I spent the bulk of the day unpacking boxes. When the house was practically box free, we stopped. Even though David had traveled all over the world, this was his first visit to Chattanooga. I didn't want it to be spent working. I'd promised him a tour of the city. Relatively new to the area myself, I enlisted Dixie to serve as tour guide. Add to the fact that Dixie was fearless when it came to scaling Chattanooga's mountains, it seemed like a great fit.

We met Dixie at one of my favorite restaurants downtown. A former woolen mill, the restaurant was an industrial spot on the water, full of charm and character. On the weekends, it was packed for brunch and one-dollar mimosas.

The weather was unseasonably warm and perfect for sitting outside.

David stretched. "I love the weather." He tilted his face toward the sky and extended his arms. "It's drab and gray in New York right now."

"You should see it in about a month. The Bartlett pear trees will be blooming, and it's absolutely beautiful—unless you have allergies, in which case it's misery."

David shook his head. "No allergies."

"Great, then you should come down and visit your mom and I'll take you up to Dollywood and show you around more of the South."

We filled Dixie in on our meeting with Dallas Simpson while we munched on spinach artichoke dip and sweet potato chips.

She listened with rapt attention. When we finished, she glanced over her glass at me. "Have you told Red?"

I took a drink of my tea to buy myself some time to respond. "Not yet, but I will."

Dixie's silence spoke volumes.

Thankfully, the waiter brought our food and gave us something else to focus on. When we finished eating, Dixie gave David the grand tour of the city, including a trek up Lookout Mountain. Unlike me, David enjoyed the ascent and actually pulled out his phone and snapped some pictures. I closed my eyes. While one hand gripped the door handle, I kept the other on my rosary. I recited the rosary over and over until I felt the car level out and we were once again on even ground.

Dixie drove back downtown to our car before she made the return trip back up the mountain. That woman had nerves of steel. She waved as she left. My legs were still a bit wobbly, so David and I stayed downtown and enjoyed a drink to give my nerves a chance to settle.

Instead of going back inside the same restaurant, we crossed the bridge and went to another favorite restaurant of mine where we could, once again, sit outside and enjoy the nice weather.

I limited myself to a Diet Coke, but I knew, from experience, I would be back to normal shortly. David ordered a beer and shared pictures he'd snapped throughout Europe and Greece of mountains that made the Appalachians look like molehills. I tried to enjoy the lovely scenes and push thoughts of my son traversing such heights to the back of my mind.

David looked up from his phone and laughed. "Mom, you look positively green. Are you sure you don't want something stronger?"

"I'm fine."

We spent a pleasant hour chatting. When I was thoroughly recovered, I drove home. My phone rang just as we entered the house. David let Aggie out to take care of business while I answered. I was glad to see Stephanie's face pop up. When she found out her brother was visiting, she started a FaceTime call, and we sat on the back patio and chatted.

I couldn't help but marvel at the technology that allowed me to spend time with both of my children, despite the distance that separated us.

Once the pleasantries were over, Stephanie updated us on her progress on combating the identify thief. So far, she'd filed reports with the police and the Federal Trade Commission. She placed fraud alerts with all the credit reporting agencies, and she'd frozen all credit accounts opened by the fraudster.

"That's a lot in less than twenty-four hours. Thank you so much, dear."

"I'm determined to catch whoever did this, so I'm not done." Stephanie's face was firm.

"Great job, sis."

"How's the murder investigation going?" Stephanie asked.

We updated her on our progress, which didn't seem like much in light of the amount of work she'd accomplished, but then, moving was extremely time-consuming.

"I've got a few updates for you there too." She reached over and pulled up a notepad. "I'm sure you probably got most of this stuff from Red already, but Joe said neither Dallas nor Keri Lynn have a criminal record. In fact, the only thing I could find on Dallas was some speeding tickets."

"What kind of car does he drive?" I asked, without thinking.

Stephanie looked up for a moment. She pulled her laptop over and typed. "Uhm…white BMW." She looked up. "Why?"

"No reason. I was just curious."

She shrugged.

David leaned in so his face was in the camera. "Did you find out anything about Keri Lynn?"

She shook her head. "Apart from being the victim of bad luck, there's not much about her either."

"What do you mean?" I asked.

"Her parents died in a car accident while she was away at college." She read from her computer screen. "Dallas Simpson is her second marriage. She was pretty young when she married her first husband, barely nineteen. He was older…a lot older than her. Her first husband died suddenly—"

I opened my mouth, but before I could speak, Stephanie said, "Before you ask, he died of natural causes. He had a heart attack while driving and crashed."

I couldn't hide my disappointment, although I didn't know why. After all, Keri Lynn was the one who'd been murdered.

"This is her second business. Her first husband was a very wealthy man. He owned magazines and newspapers and had started his own production company."

"So she inherited a lot of money?"

"She inherited a million dollars from his life insurance and a café, but I didn't see that she inherited much more than that. About six months after his death, the café caught fire."

"You're right. She's had a lot of bad luck. 'Gloom, despair, and agony on me,'" I sang.

The children looked at me as though I'd lost my mind.

"You know…" I sang the rest of the verse from a song from the 1970s variety show *Hee Haw*. Unfortunately, the show was years before my children's time, and they merely stared at me.

"Yes, well. She married Dallas Simpson about five years ago." Stephanie looked up. "Wanna guess what he did before starting Pet Haven?"

"He said he was involved in security systems," I said.

David raised his hand. "But I'll bet my tiny New York apartment he wasn't the engineer creating them. I'll bet my last dollar he was in sales."

Stephanie touched her nose. "Ding. Ding. Ding. Fifty points. Well done, little brother. He sold home security systems."

David shrugged. "Actually, it's not that impressive. If you'd talked to him, you would know how much he sounded like Dad."

I was taken aback and stared at David for several minutes. "Oh my God, you're right. He sounds just like Albert when he was trying to sell used cars."

We talked a bit longer, but Stephanie didn't have anything else. She squinted and got close to the screen. "Are you two sitting outside?"

"We are indeed." David smiled. "Lounging on the deck of Mom's new house." He picked up the phone and spun it around.

"I'm so jealous. It's freezing in Chicago."

"Come on down." David smiled. "The weather is wonderful."

"I wish I could, but I was just down there a month ago." She pouted. "I thought I was going to be able to get down for a long weekend." She sat up straight. "Actually, Joe and Turbo will be there. He's going to check out a new Plott hound breeder. I planned to go with them, but one of my cases just got a lot more complicated and I've got a lot of work to do."

"I'm sorry you won't be able to come down. It would be so wonderful to have both of my children here. But tell Joe he's always welcome to stay here. I'd love to see him and Turbo, and I know Aggie would love seeing her friend too."

Turbo was Joe's K-9 police dog. He was a Plott hound, and Aggie was absolutely besotted.

I glanced over at Aggie, who had harassed David until he gave in, propped the phone against the umbrella pole in the middle of the table, and picked her up. She was now perched on his chest with her head on his shoulder. At the mention of her name, she lifted her head and her tail started to wag like the blades of a fan.

"I'll tell him, but I think he's going to stay with Red."

I scowled. "Red never mentioned a word."

"Don't be too hard on him, Mom. It was a last-minute trip. Actually, one of the other officers was supposed to go, but he got the flu, so they just asked Joe if he could go."

"Come on, sis. Sure you can't sneak away?"

Stephanie shook her head. "I doubt it. I'll know more tomorrow."

We talked for a few minutes and then ended the call.

After we hung up with Stephanie, David and I talked through what we'd learned.

"Poor Keri Lynn. She really has had a rough life." I sighed.

"She doesn't seem to have been lucky in business or lucky in love, does she?"

"I can't imagine getting married at nineteen. I was twenty-two when I married your father, and looking back, I think that was too young."

David reached over and squeezed my hand. "You two lasted a quarter of a century. That's pretty good."

I smiled. "You're right. I think the national average says most marriages only last two to five years." I thought for a moment. "Do you think Keri Lynn was one of those women who was attracted to bad boys?"

David laughed. "I don't know that I'd necessarily classify Dallas Simpson as a 'bad boy,' although he might be a bad seed."

"You mean like that old movie? *The Bad Seed.*"

He nodded. "They remade it, but the original with that little girl was scarier."

I pondered that. "I suppose he could be a bad seed." I shook my head. "It's hard for me to tell. I might be judging him because he looks and acts like a prep school gigolo."

David and I sat outside a few minutes longer, but I needed to get some rest. Tomorrow I would be working two jobs. I was going to the museum in the morning and would leave early and swing by Pet Haven. I knew finding information that might give Dallas Simpson a reason to murder his wife was a long shot. However, I needed to be on my toes. After all, if I was right, he'd already murdered once. Bad seed or not, I had no doubt he wouldn't hesitate to murder again.

Chapter 11

The next morning, David drove me to work so he could use the car. We got up early to have time to stop at Da Vinci's for coffee and pastries. I wanted to take David to the museum so I could introduce him to Linda Kay, but I got a text stating she was feeling under the weather and wouldn't be in today. In fact, she encouraged me to stay home. When I texted her that I was already at work, she told me to wrap up early and spend time with my son. I thanked her and promised I would. For probably the hundredth time since starting to work at the museum, I thanked the fates that allowed me to work for such a generous and kind woman.

Without Jacob or Linda Kay, the museum offices were quiet. I got a lot of work done, but it was also lonely. I missed our coffee and tea breaks and the small jokes and art lessons. Thinking about our little trio reminded me I needed to check on Jacob. I picked up my cell phone and called him.

"Hello, Jacob, it's Lilly Echo—"

"Lilly, thank God," he whispered.

"What's the—"

"Look, I don't have much time before she realizes I've been alone for fifteen minutes. I need you to come and get me out." He hurried. "Do you have a pen? Write down this address."

He rattled off an address and I scribbled it down. "Jacob, I don't understand. Why—"

"For God's sake, Lilly, you have to help me. I can't take much more of this." His voice quivered. "Please, I'm being tortured, and I don't know how much more I can take."

"What's going on?" I grabbed my purse and hurried to the door. "Where are you?"

"My parents' house."

I stopped. "Wait. What?"

He whimpered. "She's smothering me. It's eighty-five degrees in this house. I'm sweating like a pig. Whenever I try to do anything, she's there." He paused and whispered, "I mean _anything._ She won't even let me go to the bathroom by myself."

"I'm sure your mother just wants to make sure you're okay. You broke your ankle."

His voice rose slightly. "The doctor gave me one of those compression boots and said I can walk. I can take a shower. I can even go back to work, but _she_ won't let me move."

I placed my hand over the phone and chuckled. When I got myself together, I said, "I'm sure your mother means well."

"I know she means well, but she's smothering me." He sighed. "If you care about me at all, just get over here and get me out of here...please."

A woman's voice in the background with a bit of a shrill whine said, "Jacob dear, is that you? Are you talking to someone? You know you should be resting. Give me five minutes, and I'll bring you a nice cup of hot cocoa and some cookies. Then we can watch _Wheel of Fortune_ and later we'll play mah-jongg."

Jacob groaned. "Please, help me."

"Okay, but I don't have a car, so you'll have to wait until—"

David sent a text message notifying me he was waiting outside. "Never mind. David's here. Give me thirty minutes." I hung up.

I had no idea what I would say, or how I could help, but I could tell Jacob was on edge. Before I left, I stopped at Jacob's desk and found several books that were probably the old Hopewell diaries Linda Kay told me about. I grabbed them and stuffed them in my bag and then hurried out.

I explained the situation to David, who found it hilarious but agreed to help with the great escape. We stopped at a nearby florist and picked up a plant. I programmed the address into my phone and prayed his parents didn't live atop Lookout or Signal Mountain, although David was less concerned about the mountains and promised to drive carefully.

Thankfully, Jacob's parents lived in an older neighborhood not far from downtown. The houses were smaller, working-class homes, but they were very well maintained with mature trees.

We sat for a few moments outside and tried to think up an excuse to get Jacob out of the house, but nothing came to mind that either of us thought would be believable. Eventually, we gave up and decided to wing it.

Plant in hand, I walked up to the front door and rang the bell, followed by David.

A petite woman with curly red hair opened the door. "May I help you?"

"I'm Lilly Echosby. I work at the museum with Jacob, and this is my son, David."

She smiled and opened the door wider. "Jacob has mentioned you. You're the accountant, right?"

I nodded.

"I'm Miriam Flemings, Jacob's mother."

We shook hands. "I'm sorry to bother him…it's just that we've been struggling to get by without him at the office. No one else knows where anything is."

She smiled. "My Jacob is a hardworking young man. I'm sure he can help you, but you mustn't stay too long or let him get overtaxed."

She hurried down the hall. I followed, shedding my coat as I walked. He wasn't kidding about the temperature. The house felt like a tropical rain forest.

At the end of the hall, she opened the door. The room held a twin bed with posters from musicals plastered across the floral wallpapered walls. It had obviously been his childhood bedroom and still reflected the decorating taste of a teenager rather than the sophisticated artistry of a young man.

"Jacob, do you feel up to visitors?" his mother asked in the quiet voice people reserved for funerals.

He rolled his eyes. "Of course, Mom."

I entered the room and handed him the plant. There was a seat near the bed, and I sat down. David walked in and moved to stand by the window.

"This is my son, David."

The two men shook.

We sat in an awkward silence for a few seconds when it was obvious Mrs. Flemings intended to stay.

Jacob handed her the plant. "Can you take that? I think Lilly and David might like some coffee."

I realize that when you're hot, you're supposed to drink warm beverages, but in this heat, coffee was the last thing I wanted. However, I couldn't deny the pleading look in his eyes and nodded.

Mrs. Flemings eagerly hopped up and took the plant. "Of course." She smiled and hurried out of the room.

I looked at David, who had also removed his jacket and was wiping his forehead.

When Mrs. Flemings was gone, Jacob used his hands to lift his leg off the pillows where it was propped, and swung it around and scooted to the edge of the bed. "Okay, what's the plan?"

He had a large black compression boot with straps that went up to his knee. The boot had a heel that was chunky and looked heavy.

I stared at him. "What plan?"

"For getting me out of this sauna? Don't tell me you don't have a plan?" He looked from me to David. "Never mind." He stood. "Quick, while she's in the kitchen, David can start the motor and we can make a run for it."

It would have been funny if he hadn't been serious.

"Hold on. I didn't come here to break you out."

He stopped and stared at me. "What?"

"I just came by to check on you."

His face fell, and he flopped down on the bed. "But why not?"

"First, because you have a broken ankle." I pointed to his leg. "Second, you can't come back to work until the doctor approves it."

"The doctor said I can move. I can walk. I can even take the boot off to shower, but she won't hear of it." His eyes filled with tears. "I now know why an animal caught in a trap will gnaw off his leg to get free."

David turned toward the window to hide the smile that I saw forming on his lips.

"I can't take much more of this." He opened his arms to encompass everything. "I'm this close to gnawing off my leg." He held up fingers indicating he was about an inch from amputation.

Mrs. Flemings came back into the room with a tray. She set the tray on the dresser and turned around. She handed me a cup.

"Thank you." I declined sugar and cream and took a sip. "This is wonderful."

David accepted a cup, although Jacob declined.

We sipped our coffee in another strained silence.

"I'm a little surprised your doctor hasn't adopted the newer medical techniques." David sipped his coffee.

"What do you mean?" Mrs. Flemings perched on the edge of her chair.

"It's just that in New York, the latest medical reports show that patients recover from injuries much faster when they get fresh air."

"Are you a doctor?" she asked eagerly.

David chuckled and then held a finger to his lips. "Shh...if people think you're a doctor, they ask a lot of medical questions."

I forced myself to avoid any type of facial expressions that might give away his ruse. "That's very true." I nodded.

Mrs. Flemings's eyes stared at David with a new respect. "I understand completely, doctor. Do you want to examine him?" She quickly turned to Jacob. "Let the doctor look at your leg. Pull down your pants."

"Mom!"

"I don't think that will be necessary." David placed his cup and saucer on the dresser. "He can just remove the compression boot."

Jacob's eyes narrowed, but he unbuckled the straps on his boot.

David made a pretense of examining his ankle.

Mrs. Flemings looked over his shoulder. After he poked Jacob's leg, he turned away and winked. "Ah, yes, well, it appears to be healing very well...except—"

"Except?" Mrs. Flemings wrung her hands. "I knew it. He's trying to do too much, isn't he? I warned him."

"On the contrary. I'm not sure he's doing enough."

Her eyes were big, and her mouth hung open. "Not doing enough?"

"Yes. You don't want to coddle him. His muscles will start to atrophy, and that could end up causing more damage." He paced around the small room with his hands behind his back. "No, I recommend more exercise. He needs to move around."

"That's what the surgeon said too, but I thought it's too soon." She stared at Jacob's leg.

"My dear lady, he needs fresh air and he needs to walk. You can't make him too comfortable or he may never want to leave."

Jacob snorted.

"I recommend he get some exercise, and don't you let him get away with taking advantage of you." David smiled at Mrs. Flemings. "I can tell you're a sensitive woman. You can't let him manipulate you into fetching and carrying for him."

She nodded eagerly. "Yes, doctor."

After a few minutes, David had convinced Mrs. Flemings to lower the heat and open the window, professing there was nothing like fresh mountain air to help in the healing process.

Before we left, Mrs. Flemings asked David to review the medicines that had been prescribed to make sure they were the same ones he would have ordered for his New York patients. She practically dragged him down the hall.

Jacob and I sat in the room in silence for several moments.

Eventually, he sighed. "He's a darned good actor."

"He is."

"Thank you."

"You're welcome." I smiled. "You know, she's only doing it because she loves you."

"I know."

I stood up. "I almost forgot. I brought you some reading material." I pulled the diaries out of my purse and handed them to him.

He looked at the books. "Thank you." He looked at me. "I wanted to read more about Ruby Hopewell." He smiled.

David assured Mrs. Flemings those were the exact same medicines he would have prescribed, and I hurried him out of the house before she asked him any more medical questions or, heaven forbid, wanted him to examine her.

We laughed about the subterfuge on the drive to Pet Haven.

"You almost had me convinced you were a doctor." I laughed.

David smiled. "All part of acting. You have to behave with confidence. You have to commit. Generally, if you speak or act confident, people believe you are who you say you are."

"That's amazing. I'm sure she absolutely believes you're a doctor." I thought for a few moments. "I feel bad about deceiving Mrs. Flemings. She's just a concerned mother, and she really has Jacob's best interest at heart."

David shrugged. "I know, which is why I didn't say anything contrary to the doctor's orders."

We talked about David and Mrs. Flemings until we arrived at the gate. Security had been given our names, and we were immediately buzzed in. David drove to the same parking space we had used the previous day.

Inside, we were greeted by the same girl from the previous day, Madison. Given the large smile she gave David, I wondered whether it was a coincidence or whether she'd arranged to be here at the same time. David seemed equally pleased, but it might be part of his technique for getting into character.

I was shown to a small office with a computer. There were two accounting ledgers on the desk. I suppressed a sigh while I sat behind the desk.

"Mr. Simpson had to step out to take care of some personal matters, but he said if you needed anything, I was to help you." Madison smiled.

She and David turned to leave.

"Excuse me. I was wondering if Heather was here." I smiled.

Madison shook her head. "Sorry, she had a family emergency."

"I hope it's nothing too serious."

She shrugged. "I really don't know. I didn't talk to her, but it can't be too bad. She left her dog here."

"Is that common?" I tried to make sure my voice sounded casual and nonchalant rather than inquisitive.

"Not really...not for Heather anyway, but her dog is rather unique."

"How so?"

"She has a pit bull/Lab mix...a mutt basically. It's a rescue and is normally really calm, almost timid. Lately, she's been really aggressive. She actually tried to bite Mr. Simpson, which was weird, and she barks nonstop." She shrugged. "It's not normal for Heather to leave her here."

"Maybe her family doesn't like dogs or has allergies," David said.

"I didn't really know that Heather had any family. She certainly never spoke of them if she did." She shook her head. "However, there are a lot of places that don't like pits, and so it's possible her options were limited, especially at the last minute. Plus, it can be expensive."

"Ah...is free boarding one of the perks of working here?" I asked.

She nodded. "That and free dog treats. My dogs love the homemade biscuits."

"So does mine." I smiled, thinking about how much Aggie loved her dog bone treat.

"I think we saw the chef yesterday...Justin?" I put my purse on the desk.

Madison nodded. "Justin hasn't been here long, and I'm not sure he's a real chef. I think he's a friend of...of the family." She looked down and colored. "Mrs. Simpson hired him."

"How nice. Did she run into him at one of the dog shows?"

Madison looked uncomfortable and avoided making eye contact.

"I went to my first dog show just the other day and was amazed at how many people specialize in making food, clothes, and jewelry for dogs."

Madison smiled. "I think it's a big business. Well..." She waved her hand around to encompass Pet Haven. "This business certainly seems to be doing well."

David surprised me by coming over and giving me a kiss on the cheek. He was affectionate, but the gesture seemed out of place. As he drew away he whispered, "Cameras."

My eyes discreetly scanned the room. At the top of the bookshelf, I saw a small object I'd assumed was a paperweight but realized was a hidden camera.

Madison and David left me alone with the ledgers and the camera.

I tried to ignore the camera but knew my gaze was drawn to it. It took several minutes before I could focus on the numbers before me. Eventually, I put the camera out of my mind and set to work.

Two hours later, I had a crick in my neck and the beginning of a headache. The computer on the desk was an ancient relic that had, undoubtedly, been set up purely for my benefit. It had a stand-alone copy of a cheap accounting software program, and the machine wasn't connected to a network or the Internet.

I stood and stretched. I was in need of the facilities, and it took everything in me not to announce to the camera that I needed the restroom.

I walked out and retraced my steps to the front desk, where I found David and Madison, heads together, sitting and going through photos. "I'm sorry, but can you show me where the bathroom is?"

"Of course." She hopped up and turned to David. "I'll be right back."

Madison led me down a hallway, where I found the door I needed and took care of business. On the way back, I deliberately took a wrong turn and wandered around. I walked down a corridor I didn't remember seeing on my first visit. I heard the faint sound of a dog barking. I followed the sound until I came to a door where the barking was much louder. There was definitely an unhappy dog behind the door. I couldn't tell if the dog was in pain or not, but he was definitely in distress. I tried the knob, but the door was locked. There was a pad to the side for a thumbprint scan.

I was curious what a dog kennel would store that would need to be secured with a thumbprint scanner. Surely a thumbprint scanner would only be needed to secure government secrets or dangerous chemicals, but before I could come up with too many answers, a security guard came up to me.

"Can I help you?" He was an older man with white hair, glasses, and a small frame. He was thin and somewhat frail and reminded me of Barney Fife from *The Andy Griffith Show*. I recognized him from the night Red and I arrived to pick up Aggie.

"I'm lost. I was hoping to find a vending machine or a break room where I could get a beverage." I smiled the friendliest smile I had.

He turned. "Follow me."

I had no choice but to obey.

He led me back the way I'd come. The door near the ladies' room led to a break room complete with a refrigerator, microwave, and vending machines.

I smiled, but Barney Fife gave a barely perceptible nod, turned, and walked out.

Unfortunately, I hadn't thought to bring my purse, so I didn't have money to get anything out of the vending machines. Ever conscious of the cameras, which I now saw were placed throughout the building, I patted my pockets. At the risk of looking like a pantomime, I gave myself the *You Could Have Had a V8* head smack and walked out.

Back in my makeshift office, I returned to the ledgers and struggled to make sense of what I was looking at. I tried not to make a mental judgment of Dallas and Keri Lynn based on the condition of their books. No matter how many times I'd heard people say they did their own accounting, I was still amazed. I knew people thought accounting was nothing more than debits and credits. They assumed if they could balance their checkbook, they could handle the accounting of their business in much the same way. However, most people didn't depreciate their household assets for tax purposes. There were laws about employee wages, unemployment, and Social Security. Unless I was mistaken, it didn't appear the Simpsons were taking out nearly enough taxes.

"Mom." David shook my arm, and I nearly jumped out of my chair.

"You scared the daylights out of me." I patted my heart to slow its thumping.

"Sorry, but I called you three times." He smiled. "Those figures must be engrossing. It's nearly five."

I took a few deep breaths. "It can't be." I looked at my watch. He was right. "Where on earth did the time go?" I collected my purse. I picked up the ledger, but Dallas Simpson had made arrangements.

Madison frowned. "I'm sorry, but Mr. Simpson gave strict instructions that none of the books are to leave the property."

"No problem." I returned the book to the desk and smiled. "I'll come back over the weekend, if that's okay."

She nodded. "I'll be working tomorrow. I'm sure that will be fine." She looked eagerly at David.

We walked out together and waved at Madison. Neither one of us spoke until we'd driven through the gate and were completely off Pet Haven property.

"How'd it go?" I glanced at David.

He smiled, but there was a glint in his eyes that made me doubt if it was related to discovering if Dallas Simpson murdered his wife or if it was more to do with a certain bright-eyed, dark-haired kennel assistant. "I find it interesting that the man, who agreed to our coming so I could observe him, didn't show up."

"Agreed. I mean, how many family emergencies can one family have?"

He shrugged. "Maybe it's all the same family member?"

"Maybe, but all of those cameras are freaky." I shuddered.

David drove home, and I was pleasantly surprised to see Red's truck in the driveway. He had thoughtfully angled the car so David and I could get in the garage.

I was puzzled not to see anyone sitting in the car. We climbed the stairs and went inside. I went to get Aggie so I could let her out. When I got to the back door, I saw Red and Joe sitting at the patio table drinking beer. "Well, isn't this cozy."

Aggie nearly leapt out of my arms at the sight of her friend Turbo, Joe's service dog. I put her down and the two ran down the stairs to play in the grass.

I hugged Joe. "Stephanie only told us you were coming last night. When did you get here?"

Joe Harrison was a handsome Lighthouse Dunes police officer with strikingly vibrant blue eyes. He wore his hair cut short in a fashion common to ex-military and men in law enforcement.

He looked at his watch. "I got here about two hours ago."

"You drove?" I asked.

He nodded. "It was a last-minute thing."

"Have you two met?" I pointed to Red and David.

"Joe introduced us." David used his beer bottle to point and both men acknowledged that introductions were made by clinking their bottles.

"Sit down." Red rose to stand, but I waved him back down.

"I'm going to change clothes." I walked back into the house but turned and came back. "How did you two get back here?"

Red smiled. "You have two law enforcement officers here. There are very few places we can't get into." He laughed.

I tilted my head and stared. "Are you serious?"

Red pointed to the side of the house. "When I was here the other day, I noticed your gate latches from the outside." He pulled a screwdriver from his pocket. "I planned to change that for you."

I changed out of my work clothes and into a pair of jeans and a casual top and then went back outside. This time, when I went out, I noticed at the foot of the first level of the deck, there was a large gas grill. "Where did that come from?" I looked around.

Joe and David both pointed to Red.

He shrugged. "Housewarming gift."

I teared up and gave him a hug. "It's beautiful, but…"

"You don't like it?" He pulled away and stared into my eyes.

"It's not that. I love it. It's just I haven't had time to go to the grocery store."

Joe laughed and bent down and slid out a cooler he had been using as a footrest. "We came bearing gifts." He opened the lid.

Inside the cooler were steaks, corncobs, beer, wine coolers, and ice.

"You thought of everything." I looked at Red.

He shrugged. "A man's got to eat."

Red took the steaks inside and prepared them for the grill. After a few minutes, I followed him in and took a few moments to show him how much I appreciated the grill and his thoughtfulness.

After a few moments, he pulled away. "Wow. If I knew a grill would get that kind of response, I'd have gotten you one sooner." He fanned himself. "In fact, I might bring another one tomorrow."

I gave him a playful swat.

He laughed. "Now, you better give me a moment to compose myself or we're never going to eat."

I got the dishes and silverware together while he prepped the food. Then he went outside and cooked.

The food smelled delicious. Aggie and Turbo were interested in the grill, but Red was adept at keeping things moving. Before long, the food was ready and we all sat down and enjoyed dinner.

The steaks were huge, and I wasn't able to eat all of mine, but Red finished it off for me. When we were done, we all sat around and talked while we drank.

Joe talked about the Plott hound puppies he hoped to see tomorrow. David entertained them by talking about our trip to visit Jacob at his parents' house. However, the conversation eventually wandered to the murder investigation.

"Any more news on Keri Lynn?" I asked.

Red shook his head. "According to her husband, he expects her back sometime this weekend."

"Really? You talked to Dallas? We didn't see him at Pet Haven—" David must have realized too late he'd said too much.

I don't know if it was due to the way I tried to shake my head without moving any part of my body or if it was the mental telepathy I was sending through my eyes to tell him to stop talking.

Red glanced from David to me and I forced my lips to smile, although I could tell it came out more like a grimace. "You went to Pet Haven?"

I took a drink of my wine cooler and frantically racked my brain for a response that wouldn't cause the vein to pulse on the side of his head. However, by the way he was pinching his nose, I knew the vein had started to pulse.

I took a deep breath. "We did go to Pet Haven…twice."

He rubbed the back of his neck. "I can't believe you went back to that place." He glanced over at David. "You let her go?"

Before David could speak, I intervened. "We went together. So I wasn't alone." He seemed about to speak, so I raised a hand and hurried on. "We went together so I wasn't alone. Besides, most of your fellow law enforcement people don't even believe he murdered his wife. And he wasn't even there today." I folded my arms across my chest.

He stared at me in silence and I defiantly met his glance.

Joe and David looked at the table, and after a few moments, their bodies started to shake. Eventually, they weren't able to contain their amusement and they both laughed out loud. I scowled at Red and he glared back at me.

Joe finally stopped laughing long enough to say, "Let me give you a piece of advice." He stared at Red. "I've learned it's easier to just give in to these Echosby women. You will never win an argument with them."

David nodded. "That's true. You'd probably have to arrest them to stop them."

Joe shook his head. "Actually I tried that, but it didn't work."

I looked at him and noticed the way his lips twitched. Eventually, I laughed too.

Red took longer to come around and sat in silence.

Joe looked from Red to me. "Okay, what did you find out at Pet Haven?"

I made a point of looking at Joe and not Red while I told him about volunteering to do the books so I could find out about their financial state. I think I noticed a look of respect in his eyes as I talked.

"For a company with so many technological advances, I'm surprised their books are so antiquated."

"What do you mean?" Joe asked.

I talked about the gated entry, security cameras, and guards. However, I could tell that I hadn't made an impression with him.

Red took a drink and turned to Joe. "Twenty-four-hour CCT footage on all areas of the building with automatic backup for all video feeds to a central server. There are thumbprint keypads on all employee areas." He took another drink. "It's pretty high-tech for a dog kennel."

"Did you look at the camera footage?" Joe asked.

Red shook his head. "Apparently, the footage got corrupted when they uploaded it to their offsite servers."

Joe smirked. "That was convenient."

Red shrugged. He talked about motion-activated sensors, night vision enhanced cameras, and a lot of gobbledygook that sounded like Greek to me. David and Joe both nodded, so I guessed it made sense to them. When he finished, he turned to me.

Red shook his head. "It's a bit over the top for a dog kennel, but the owner, Dallas Simpson, is a bit over the top."

David described Dallas Simpson's white designer clothes, super tanned skin, and highlights. Joe and Red got a big laugh as David described how Aggie licked off his spray tan.

When the laughter died down, I continued, "So with all the security and cameras and…whatever, I expected they would at least have an up-to-date accounting system that was linked to their bank account and allowed mobile access and digital upload of receipts. I mean, even the museum has moved away from handwritten ledgers."

"That does seem strange, but there are a lot of people who like gadgets and electronics but don't know anything about accounting." Joe yawned.

"I know, but it's more than that."

"Maybe he just put the ledgers there for you. Maybe there's a completely different system," Red said.

I sighed. "I don't think so." I struggled to find the right words to explain. "Why go to all that effort? He couldn't have known I'd volunteer to do this before yesterday." I stared at Red. "These books go back to the beginning of the year."

"So, did you find anything?" Red asked.

I thought for several moments. "They've spent a ton of money, too much money. I don't see that they can possibly bring in enough to cover the expenses. In fact, it looks like they're in the hole pretty deep. The marble entry and the security, the chef and masseuse—"

Joe choked and started to cough. When he finally collected himself, he stared at me. "Chef? Masseuse? For dogs?"

Joe, Red, and I all nodded.

Joe yawned and then looked at Turbo, who had worn himself out chasing Aggie around the yard and was sprawled at Joe's feet. "Wow, Turbo, you're being neglected." He petted the dog. "You want a massage, boy?"

I leaned forward. "I think that's a great idea."

He nearly fell out of his seat. "The Lighthouse Dunes K-9 unit expense budget won't extend to massages for the police, let alone the dogs," he joked.

I scooted to the edge of my seat. "I would pay for it. I was thinking about taking Aggie to day care tomorrow when I go to work on the books."

"Tomorrow?" Red exploded. "You're not going back there."

"Yes, I am. I have to. I said I would get the books ready for the end of year and I'm not done." He looked ready to speak and I hurried on. "Before you ask, I offered to take the books home, but Dallas Simpson gave strict instructions nothing was to be removed."

He took a few deep breaths and calmed himself.

Joe looked from me to Red. Eventually, he shrugged. "If you're going back, then it might be a good idea to take Turbo and Aggie with you." He yawned.

The air was still and the night was quiet. Red stared at his friend.

Joe shrugged. "She's going whether you want her to or not." He paused to let his comment soak in. "Besides, if she has David with her, he can keep an eye on her."

David leaned forward. "It'll be broad daylight and there will be tons of people around." He said quietly, "I'm not going to let anything happen to my mom."

Joe leaned forward. "Aggie may be small, but she's a fierce little thing and has risked her life to defend Lilly before." He looked at Turbo. "Plus, I pity the fool who would lay a hand on either of them with Turbo around."

Joe and Red stared into each other's eyes. Some conversation transpired without one word being spoken. Eventually, Red nodded.

The tension went down slightly, but the air was still filled with static.

David grinned and rubbed his hands together. "Great. Now, what's the plan?"

Chapter 12

We talked a bit longer, but Joe's yawns grew more frequent and his eyelids drooped. The poor man had driven six hundred miles and was exhausted. David, Joe, and Turbo walked to Red's truck together. Red hung back.

When we were alone, he turned to me. "Look, I know you're an adult… an independent woman, and you're free to make your own decisions." He looked at me and released a sigh. "I also know I can come across as controlling, but it's only because I want you to be safe. I care about you, and I don't like the idea of you deliberately hanging around a murder suspect."

I opened my mouth to object, but he placed a finger over my lips.

"Wait." He paused and took a deep breath. "I know what you're going to say. You don't need my permission to do anything. You're capable of taking care of yourself, and I have no right to interfere." He released a big breath. "That's all true, and I'm working on not being controlling."

I waited. "May I speak now?"

He nodded.

"I wasn't going to say any of that. What I was going to say was that I appreciate the fact you want me to be safe. I know your heart's in the right place. It's just part of your nature to want to protect. From your military service to law enforcement, it's in you and I appreciate that." I leaned up and kissed him. "So, thank you. However, I have to do what I think is right." I sighed and took a minute to find the right words. "I saw a woman murdered. I barely knew her, but she deserved more than to have her life taken from her." I paused. "I raised my kids to do the right thing. I raised them to follow the Golden Rule and treat others the way they want to be treated. If someone murdered…" My eyes filled with water and I had to take a moment to catch my breath. "If something happened to Stephanie or David, I hope that if anyone saw something, they would come forward. If they could help, then they would." I sniffed. "Too many people don't want to get involved. I don't want to be one of those people."

He hugged me tightly for a few moments.

I jumped when the screen door slammed. David sidled past. "Sorry, I didn't mean to interrupt, but—"

I wiped my eyes. "It's okay, come in."

Red kissed my forehead. He offered his hand to David. "It was nice meeting you." They shook. "I need to go. I don't want to have to carry Joe inside when we get to the house."

He left and I watched as he backed out of the driveway and drove away before I closed the door.

David helped load the dishwasher. Before he went to bed, he looked at me. "I like Red. He seems like a nice guy."

I stared at him.

"You deserve a nice guy." He kissed me on the cheek, turned around, and walked to his bedroom.

My feet were frozen in place. After what felt like a minute, I smiled, scooped up Aggie, and went to bed.

The next day I woke up early and made a quick run to a nearby grocery store and picked up bacon, eggs, and a few other necessities. David was still asleep when I returned. By the time I finished cooking breakfast, he was up. We ate and discussed plans for our trip to Pet Haven. I wasn't sure if Red had discouraged Joe from helping me sleuth until the doorbell rang. I was pleasantly surprised to see both Joe and Turbo.

I craned my neck around Joe, but Red was nowhere in sight. Joe explained that Red had planned to come with us this morning, but he had gotten a call and had to leave at the last minute. He said he'd join us later.

I struggled to keep the disappointment I felt from showing on my face, but my smile felt fake, even to me.

Aggie was thrilled to have her buddy and would have been content to play "catch me if you can" all day. However, that wasn't the plan.

Joe and Turbo followed David, Aggie, and me over to Pet Haven. He said he wanted to see this place with his own eyes. However, I wondered if he didn't feel comfortable leaving his best friend in my care. Regardless, we made our way to Pet Haven.

At the gate, I gave all of our names and explained that my daughter's boyfriend's dog would be joining Aggie for day care today.

The guard must have accepted my explanation because the gate swung open and we were both allowed to drive onto the property.

David, Aggie, and I waited for Joe and Turbo to get out of the car. We all walked in together.

I could tell by the look in Joe's eyes, he was impressed by the facility. He stood at the counter and took in the luxurious details.

Once again, Madison was there. She smiled broadly as I introduced her to Joe and Turbo. I explained that my daughter's boyfriend and his dog were here for a short time and that I'd told them how nice the facility was and wanted Turbo and Aggie to get an opportunity to play, plus massages. I assured her I expected to pay.

She typed on the computer and told me there was a grooming, massage, and private play package on sale today.

When she told me the amount, I nearly passed out. Instead, I forced a fake smile. "That will be fine."

Joe's eyes got as large as silver dollars.

As she was checking Aggie and Turbo in, a door opened, and Dallas Simpson walked out. He was, as always, dressed all in white. He smiled big and walked around the counter.

"Lilly, it's so good to see you again." He looked around. "Who do we have here? Don't tell me it's another son."

I smiled. "No, not exactly." I explained who Joe and Turbo were and the two men shook.

Turbo sat quietly by Joe's side, while Aggie tried to get out of my arms and over to Dallas Simpson. However, I was ready for her today and tightened my grip so she wasn't able to escape.

Dallas Simpson acted like a perky used car salesman almost every time I'd ever seen him. He looked and acted like a fake. However, today his act was even perkier. Even more used-car-salesman-esque and even more fake. He took his already over-the-top personality and turned it up about five hundred notches.

David and I exchanged glances.

"I'm so sorry I wasn't here to greet you both yesterday, but..." He waved his hands. "Family, what can I say."

I thought about it. What was there to say? In fact, I couldn't think of anything to say either. I couldn't help wishing Dixie was here. She always seemed to know the right words at the right moment. We stood in awkward silence. "How about I take you both on a tour of our beautiful, state-of-the-art facilities?" Dallas smiled.

Joe and David accepted his offer and the three of them were just about to leave when Barney Fife shuffled over and whispered something to Mr. Simpson.

A few seconds later, the front door opened and, to my surprise, in walked Red.

My initial reaction was that he'd planned this as a way of protecting me. However, one look at his face told me that wasn't the case.

Red was in full-blown law enforcement mode, and I knew his presence here had nothing to do with me. In fact, he glanced in my direction and barely nodded as he focused in on Dallas Simpson.

"You're the officer who came by the other night." He glanced at me but quickly returned his gaze to Red. "I've answered all of your questions multiple times. This is harassment, and I'm going to call my lawyer if this doesn't stop."

Red walked up to him. "Is there someplace we can talk in private?"

I expected Dallas to escort him to his office and immediately started to back up. However, he surprised me by saying, "I don't have any secrets." He spread his hands wide. "This is definitely starting to feel like harassment." He turned to me. "Mrs. Echosby has apologized and acknowledged she made a mistake, so I think it's bad taste for the police to continue to persecute me." He huffed.

In fact, I could feel his energy level rising and knew an explosion was coming. I didn't have to wait long.

"My wife and I are trying to run a respectable business and you have no right to come traipsing in here, asking questions, taking pictures, and looking for evidence that doesn't exist." With each statement, his voice and gestures grew larger, to the point that his arms were flailing so much he looked like he was trying to land a plane. Some of the workers in the day care room had stopped and walked closer to the lobby to see what the commotion was about.

Red stood still, but I noticed the vein on the side of his head pulse.

Joe and Turbo had also grown still and yet, they seemed more alert than they had moments earlier.

Dallas ranted on for several moments. He threatened to contact the mayor, write letters to his golf partner who was neighbors with several state representatives, and finished with his attorney who would sue the state of Tennessee, the TBI, the police department, and Red personally.

When he stopped for a breath, Red said quietly, "I'm sorry to inform you there's been an accident."

Dallas's face went from red to stark white. "An accident? Who?"

"I'm sorry to inform you that your wife was killed in a car accident on her way back from Georgia." He paused. "I'm very sorry for your loss."

Dallas let out a scream and then collapsed onto the floor.

Chapter 13

Red ordered Madison to get some water. He then worked to revive Dallas.

Madison returned with the water. Several of the kennel workers had come out to watch.

I turned to Madison. "Is the vet onsite today?"

She nodded.

"Go get him," Red ordered.

She hurried to the back and returned quickly with a short, brown-skinned man with jet-black hair and glasses.

"I'm Dr. Patel." He squatted next to Dallas. "What happened?"

"He received a shock and fainted." Red squatted nearby.

Dr. Patel went to work. He lifted Dallas's eyelids and checked his pulse. He turned to Red. "Help me get him to the back."

Red stood up from a squatted position and bent over. He reached underneath the back of Dallas's knees and pushed his legs backward so his feet were tucked up against his butt and his knees were in the air. He grabbed Dallas's left wrist and pulled him forward. With legs spread wide, Red lowered his left shoulder and bent down. This move allowed Dallas's upper torso to fall over his back. He grabbed one of Dallas's legs and then stood up. He shifted the man's dead weight slightly so it was balanced. The entire maneuver took less than ten seconds. When he was upright, he followed the doctor to the back. Red walked upright and didn't appear to feel any strain, even with Dallas wrapped around his shoulders like a fur stole.

Several of the workers stood nearby, mouths open, and shock registered on their faces. They looked unsure of what to do.

Joe moved forward. "I think you should all go back to work. Mr. Simpson will be well taken care of."

Madison nodded. "He's right."

Slowly everyone returned to what they were doing. That left, David, Joe, and me in the lobby with Madison.

She took a few deep breaths but was obviously shaken up.

David stepped forward. "You're looking a bit peaked yourself." He placed an arm around her back. "Let's get you a cup of coffee or tea."

She hesitated and glanced back at the reception area.

David glanced at me. "My mom can fill in."

I nodded. "You go in the back and take a few moments. I'll look after things here." I smiled.

She nodded gratefully and allowed David to escort her to the back.

I walked behind the counter and sat down.

One of the workers returned and walked to the desk. She had a card in her hand. "Are these the two dogs for the spa package?"

I exchanged a glance with Joe, who shrugged. I wasn't sure how long Red would be or whether or not Madison would be in any shape to continue working. I turned to the girl. "Yes. This is Aggie." I handed the poodle to her. Then I turned to Joe.

He handed over Turbo's leash, but before he gave it to her, he said, "He isn't to play with any other dogs, just Aggie."

She smiled and escorted the dogs away.

Joe looked at his watch.

"You don't have to stay. I know you need to go meet with the breeder."

"Are you sure?"

I nodded. "I'm just going to sit here and smile and greet whoever walks through that door. You go!"

He left and I looked at the scheduling computer. It appeared to be a glorified calendar. Only one person came in during the few minutes while I sat there, a man in a business suit with a dog I recognized as a shih tzu. The dog's name was Lester. I saw from the calendar Lester had an appointment for day care and grooming. The dog looked bored, and his owner looked impatiently at his watch. I wasn't sure what button triggered the workers to come out, so I smiled and extended my hands. His owner deposited the bundle of fluff in my arms, turned, and walked out, muttering something about his wife picking up the dog later.

Lester and I sat at the desk and waited for Madison or someone else to come back. If no one came, I would have to leave the front desk and take him back myself. As we sat, I got a text message from Dixie. I shifted the dog so both thumbs were free and I was able to respond. I quickly updated her on the latest news about Keri Lynn and even managed to take a selfie of Lester and me.

Dixie confirmed he was a shih tzu, which she said was one of the toy breeds. Before I could respond, the back door opened and Red came out.

"Is this where you've been working?"

I explained that Madison was shaken up and David took her to the back. He nodded.

"Red, it can't be Keri Lynn in the car. I mean, how could it be?" I shook my head. "It can't be Keri Lynn. I saw him." I looked around to make sure no one was listening. I leaned close and whispered, "I saw him strangle her."

He shook his head. "She's on camera. She stopped for gas and used her credit card. We have eyewitness testimony who confirmed it was Keri Lynn Simpson driving."

"But…how is that possible?"

The back door opened, and David and Madison came out. Her color was closer to normal, but she still looked a bit wobbly.

"I can take over from here." She extended her arms.

I stood up and handed over Lester. She swiped the screen and, within seconds, the back door opened and the same person who had taken Turbo and Aggie came out and collected Lester.

Madison sat down. She forced a smile that never made it to her eyes. "Thank you."

"Are you sure you're up to working? I can stay. I came to work today and I'm fine with sitting here if you give me a quick training on how to work your fancy system."

This time the smile did reach her eyes. "Thank you, Mrs. Echosby, but I'm fine."

"Please call me Lilly." I glanced at David, who was hovering nearby.

"I'm going to sit out here with her and then I can take her home. I don't think she should be driving."

I hid a smile and nodded.

"Why don't you take Lilly's car? I'll drive your mom home."

I had forgotten Red was standing there until he spoke. I turned to look at him.

"If that's okay with you?" he asked.

I nodded and turned back to Madison. "Are you sure there's nothing I can do?"

She shook her head.

I turned to leave but quickly turned back to Madison. "What about Turbo and Aggie?"

"No worries, Mom. I'll bring them home."

I asked Madison if it would be okay if I paid for the services in advance, and she assured me I could. She then took my credit card and processed the transaction.

Red and I left together. Once we were in the car, I noticed he wasn't driving toward my house.

Before I could ask, he said, "Let's grab lunch, and I can fill you in."

I looked at my watch and noticed it was a lot later than I realized. It was only when I saw the time that I realized how hungry I was. My stomach reinforced the realization by growling.

"I'll take that growl as a yes." Red grinned and drove to one of the new restaurants in town that we'd talked about trying but hadn't yet made it to.

The restaurant wasn't crowded, so we were able to be seated immediately.

We took care of the important business first. We ordered beverages and scanned the menu. When our waiter returned, we placed our orders. Once those decisions were completed, we were able to focus.

"What happened?"

Red took a sip of the coffee he'd ordered. "I got a call from the state police about the accident. One of the officers remembered I'd been asking questions about Keri Lynn Simpson, so when the accident was reported, they called me."

"But what happened to cause the accident?"

He shrugged. "She left Georgia on her way back to Chattanooga early this morning. She must have wanted to avoid rush hour traffic in Atlanta, so she timed her departure accordingly." He sighed. "She never made it out of Georgia." He tapped the table with his fork. "Apparently she'd been visiting a sick relative in rural Georgia. We don't know for sure. The traffic investigators will have to take a close look to tell us exactly what happened. However, best guess at the moment is she was in the mountains and came around a corner too quickly. Sometimes the fog settles on the mountain and those roads can be slippery." He shrugged. "We think she lost control of her car and the car careened over the side of the mountain."

"That's horrible." Visions of Dixie traveling up Lookout Mountain made my eyes fill with tears.

Red slid a handkerchief toward me.

I cried. "I don't know why I'm crying. I barely knew that woman. It's just…I worry about Dixie driving up Lookout Mountain."

Red was well aware of how afraid I was of driving in the mountains and didn't say anything. He merely reached out and gave my hand a squeeze.

"I just don't understand how this can be. I mean, are they sure it was Keri Lynn?"

Red nodded. "I had one of the troopers take a look at the camera footage from the gas station." He nodded. "It was definitely her."

"What's wrong?" I looked at him.

"Nothing." He rubbed the back of his neck and the scar that covered one side of his face pulsed.

"You didn't get in trouble for looking into this, did you?" I waited.

"I'll be fine."

I could tell by the look in his eyes and the red tint that traveled up his neck that he was lying.

I waited.

Eventually, he sighed. "Dallas is claiming I've been harassing him. I've been ordered to stay away. My boss thinks…he thinks I'm biased."

He didn't need to tell me I was the one who was accused of creating the bias.

He looked up. "It'll be fine. Really."

My brain felt like mush. Thoughts raced around, but I wasn't able to connect them into complete sentences. Keri Lynn had been alive this morning.

Our lunch arrived. The hunger I felt just a few short minutes ago had vanished, and the sight and smell of food made me want to gag. I excused myself and found the ladies' room.

I took several deep breaths and splashed my face with cold water. After a few minutes, the wave of nausea I'd felt earlier passed and I went back to the table.

During my absence, Red had had the waiter box up both of our meals, so when I returned to the table, I was staring at a Styrofoam box.

I mouthed a thank-you and he nodded as we left.

He didn't say much during the ride home, other than to ask if I needed him to stop anywhere.

He pulled up to the house. "Are you sure you're okay? Do you need me to get you anything?"

I shook my head. "No. I'm sorry. I didn't mean to ruin your lunch."

"You know I don't care about that."

It took a little work, but I was finally able to convince him I was fine. It wasn't long after he left that I got a text from Dixie. She was in the area. I made tea and she was at the house by the time it finished brewing.

We sat outside on the patio and drank in silence for several minutes. Eventually, she turned to me. "I can't take this. What happened?"

I told her all that I knew and sat silent.

"Okay, so now what?"

I stared, confused. "What do you mean?"

"What are we going to do now? You can't just give up." She stared at me as though I was a stranger and she was trying to remember my name.

"There's nothing more to do. Obviously, I was wrong. Obviously, I'm a crazy woman who is hallucinating and no one, especially Red, will ever believe me again." I turned my head away so she couldn't see the tears that were about to overflow.

That was when she smacked the back of my head.

"Ouch!" I turned to face her. "What did you do that for?"

"Well, somebody had to smack some sense into you." She grinned. "Might as well be me."

I stared at her openmouthed for several moments. Eventually, laughter bubbled up inside me.

We both laughed. We laughed long and hard. When one of us stopped, we looked at each other and started all over again. Eventually, we pulled ourselves together.

"I can't believe you did that." I rubbed the back of my head.

"Well, you were talking like a crazy woman, so I had to do something."

"I'm not talking crazy. It's the truth."

"First off, you are not crazy and you don't have hallucinations—"

"But—"

"Don't but me. Lilly Ann Echosby, I've known you for close to thirty years. You're an intelligent woman. You're not crazy. My aunt Constance, who believed her brain was a radio transmitter that she could use to talk to aliens in outer space, was crazy. My uncle Horatio, who liked to run around the neighborhood buck naked in the middle of the winter and tried to dig his way to China, was crazy." She pointed at me. "You are intelligent and caring, and you've got a mind as sharp as a meat cleaver. So, stop wallowing in self-pity and turn on that brain and let's figure this thing out."

I looked at my friend and struggled to find the right words. "Dixie, I appreciate the faith you have in me, but I can't…I don't know what you're saying."

She sighed. "Look, I'm saying you're not crazy." She looked at me expectantly.

"Okay, maybe crazy was a bit of an exaggeration. Maybe delusional would be more accurate."

She reached over and smacked me again.

"Ouch." I rubbed the back of my head. "Now, what was that for?"

"I'm trying to get your brain to reset because right now, it's stuck on stupid."

"Thanks."

"You're welcome." She huffed. After a long pause she said, "Look, remember what Sherlock Holmes said?"

"Elementary?"

"Stop being daft." She looked up and clucked her tongue. "Once you take away the impossible, whatever's left is the truth."

I smiled. "Once you eliminate the impossible, whatever remains, no matter how improbable, must be the truth."

"Yeah, that's it. So do it." She stared at me. "Eliminate the impossible."

I stared at her for several minutes.

"Do I need to smack you again?" She raised her hand.

I held up my hands in surrender. "Okay. Okay." I thought.

"I'll start. You're not crazy." She held up her hand and ticked off each item. "You're not hallucinating. Nor are you delusional."

I nodded. "Then, that means..." I stared at her.

She nodded. "That means you actually saw someone get murdered."

"But how can that be? If Keri Lynn died this morning, that would have to mean..."

She nodded. "Exactly."

"It wasn't Keri Lynn I saw murdered. It had to be someone else..." The realization hit me. I stared at Dixie. "Heather?"

"Who?"

"Heather. She worked at Pet Haven. She had long blond hair. She looked a lot like Keri Lynn." I was so excited I was talking quickly. "Oh my God. She's the one I thought was having an affair with Dallas." I thought back to the video. "Oh my God, it had to be Heather because of the watch."

"Okay, now you've lost me. What watch?"

"I knew something was off."

"You kept saying something seemed off, but I still don't understand."

"It's the watch. When I saw Keri Lynn at the dog show, she was wearing an expensive watch, a diamond Rolex. Dallas has a matching one. But the woman on the video wasn't wearing an expensive watch. She had on a cheap plastic watch. But it was the arm. She had the watch on the wrong arm. Keri Lynn was left-handed. Left-handed people almost always wear a watch on their right arms. The woman I saw murdered had her watch on her left hand. So..."

"She was right-handed."

I nodded. "Exactly, and Heather was right-handed. I remember her mentioning it." I smacked my forehead. "How could I be so stupid? She also wasn't wearing the fancy wedding ring Keri Lynn had. The woman I saw murdered didn't have a ring on."

"What about the man?"

I took a moment to think. "He was wearing a watch, a big, fancy, expensive watch." I smiled.

Dixie smacked the table. "We need to call Red and let him know."

I shook my head. "Not yet."

"Why not?"

I sighed. "Look, Red went out on a limb for me. He went to Pet Haven and accused Dallas of murder even though there was no body. He sent forensics teams to review the kennel, and now it looks like Keri Lynn was alive the entire time." I stared at Dixie. "I can't turn around now and say, 'Oh, I made a mistake. It was Heather I saw murdered and not Keri Lynn' with no other proof than the fact she wasn't wearing a wedding ring and had her watch on her right arm. They'll make him a laughingstock."

"Okay, so we need to get proof."

"Madison said Heather had a family emergency and she's been gone since Sunday."

"Convenient. Does that make Dallas a serial killer?"

"We don't know that he killed his wife. According to Red, she was in the car alone. Unless..."

"What? I can see the wheels turning."

"Unless he drove up to Georgia and did something to her car."

"Something like what?"

I shook my head. "Beats me. I don't know anything about cars. But I remember seeing something on television, I think it was on *Murder, She Wrote*." I paused to try to remember exactly which show it was, but I couldn't and gave up. "Anyway, the killer knew his victim had to drive down a really steep mountain drive with lots of curves and turns. So he cut some kind of rod."

"What happened?"

I thought back. "I think the car worked fine at first, but then, after a while, the rod thingy broke and the driver couldn't control the car around the turns. It went over a cliff into the ocean."

"Do we know if Dallas Simpson knows anything about cars? He doesn't strike me as the type to get his hands dirty."

"I don't know."

"But if she was in Georgia and he was in Chattanooga, would he have had the time to do it?"

"Good questions." I thought things over. "I guess we need to figure out how far away she was, but..." I turned to stare at my friend. "He was supposed to be at Pet Haven yesterday. David and I were supposed to meet him." She already knew about my plan to volunteer to do the books, so I filled her in on David asking to shadow him for a role he was going to play. "Everything was all arranged, but when we arrived yesterday, we were told he had a family emergency and had to leave."

"So he had the opportunity."

I nodded.

"If that's true, he's killed two women." She looked at me. "How many people do you have to murder before you're considered a serial killer?"

"I have no idea."

"Why do you suppose he did it?"

"Maybe Heather wanted him to leave his wife. Maybe Keri Lynn found out he was having an affair." I picked up my phone and quickly typed a text message.

"What?"

"I just suggested David invite Madison to dinner tonight."

"Madison?"

I forgot Dixie didn't know Madison, so I explained who she was and that I thought there were a few sparks going between her and David. My phone vibrated, and I looked at the message.

"What's that smile?"

"It's David. He said he already invited her." I smiled. David and I always had been connected.

"Great, so what now?"

"Now I need you to take me to the grocery store."

Chapter 14

I sent text messages to Red and Joe inviting them to the house for dinner. Dixie got the bright idea of inviting the other members from her dog class, so I sent messages to them too. I was surprised that all of them accepted, especially given the short notice. We made trips to a grocery store, a liquor store, and a bakery.

When we got home, Red's truck was in front. When we pulled into the garage, he came from the side yard.

"I fixed the latch on your gate." He held up a screwdriver.

"Thank you." I lifted the rear hatch of the SUV and reached in to get some of the bags, but he wasn't having it.

"I've got these. You unlock the door." He picked up most of the bags, which were so heavy I'd actually taken advantage of the grocery bagger's offer to load my groceries into the car. I was still amazed this was a service offered by grocery stores. In my corner of Indiana, the grocery bagger was extinct, just like gas station attendants who pumped your gas.

He hauled the bags into the house and got the serving items down from the upper shelves.

When the heavy lifting was done, it dawned on me that he should be at work. "Why aren't you working?"

He sighed. "I'm on paid leave for a few days while Internal Affairs investigates Dallas Simpson's claims."

I gasped.

"Don't worry. It's going to be fine."

"It's all my fault. I'm so sorry." I couldn't help the tears that came or the overwhelming desire to hug him, mixed with a desire to stay away since

I was the cause of the pain. Eventually, the desire to help overwhelmed everything else, and I reached out and hugged him as tightly as I could.

We stood together, holding on to each other in the middle of the kitchen. As I cried into his chest, something shifted. I wasn't clear who was comforting whom.

Dixie had gone to a nearby gas station to get ice. She walked into the kitchen. "Lilly Ann, I bought—" She stopped. "Sorry."

We pulled apart.

I sniffed and reached for a paper towel to dry my face.

"I always seem to be interrupting you two."

"You weren't interrupting anything." I blew my nose.

"Well, dagnabbit, why are you crying?" She scowled at Red, who held up both hands in a gesture of surrender. "Am I going to have to smack some sense into you again?"

I laughed. "No, you've hit me enough for one day."

Red gave me a sideways glance but wisely excused himself and went outside.

I quickly told Dixie about his paid leave.

She swore but then turned to me. "Now what?"

"Now, we have to figure out how Dallas Simpson murdered Heather and Keri Lynn and we need to do it quickly…and without Red's help."

She nodded. "Okay, then we'll need to be very careful tonight." She glanced out the back window to make sure he wasn't standing nearby. "If we're going to put your plan in motion, we're going to have to be really careful."

"I know. I'll try to keep him busy."

As it turned out, keeping Red busy and distracted wasn't a problem at all. Planning a last-minute grill/housewarming/meet-my-son/allow-me-to-pick-your-brains-for-information-to-catch-a-killer party was a lot of work.

Red not only mowed my grass; he also edged it. It was winter, and the grass was in hibernation, but the unseasonably warm weather had started the growth season earlier than usual. Plus, the house had been vacant for a while and the yard was overgrown and neglected. In addition to the yard work, he had already fixed the latch on the gate so that intruders would have to, at least, reach over the top of the five-foot wooden privacy gate to unlatch it. He wanted to include a lock, but I convinced him it wouldn't be needed. He re-keyed all of the locks in the house and garage and trimmed the hedges, which revealed a surprise.

The hedges in front of the house were so tall and overgrown that they hid a good portion of the house. When they were trimmed, they revealed a beautifully weathered piece of ironwork.

He marinated the steaks and chicken. When it seemed like he might finish a task early, Dixie or I found a new one.

Red was a tireless worker, and the yard looked amazing. All of his hard work did come at a price. I took him a cold glass of water. As he drank, an easterly wind blew and rustled the leaves. I got a whiff of a pungent odor.

I sniffed, trying to find the source. After a few seconds, I realized the origin of the odor was Red. I frowned.

He took his sweatshirt and wiped his forehead. "I know. I'm definitely ripe."

"Ah…yeah. I'm so sorry. I appreciate all of your hard work." I glanced around. "The yard looks amazing. The meat is marinating. Everything is just about ready, but…"

He nodded. "Yep. As soon as I drag these branches out of the way, I'm going to run home and take a shower."

I reached up and kissed him. "Salty." I smacked my lips and hurried out of range of his hand, which threatened to swipe my bottom.

He left to get cleaned up, promising to return soon. Dixie and I continued getting things ready.

Monica Jill was the first to arrive. She knocked on the door and came in carrying a bottle of wine and a gift bag.

"I told you on the phone you didn't need to bring anything."

She snorted. "No Southern girl arrives at a party empty-handed."

I thanked her and placed the bottle on the makeshift bar we'd made from an old chest.

David and Madison were next.

Dixie and I were standing in the living room when they pulled up. We both noted that David opened her door and that the amount of personal space separating them was minimal.

"They look good together," Dixie said.

I smiled. "Agreed. She's really nice too."

Madison was holding Aggie when she climbed out of the car. David then opened the back, and Turbo slowly climbed out of the car.

They came in and David made the introductions, although Dixie was the only person she didn't know so far.

Madison handed a freshly groomed and clean-smelling Aggie over to me. They had placed bright pink ribbons on her ears, which I was surprised she'd permitted to remain. Normally, she removed them before I could get her home from the groomers.

Aggie gave me a lick and then snuggled close to my chest.

I held her up so I could stare at her more closely. After a while, I turned to Madison. "What's wrong with my dog?"

Her eyes grew large. "What do you mean? Is something wrong?"

"There's a lot of people here, not to mention food." I waved a hand to a tray of hors d'oeuvres nearby. "Aggie should be barking and running in circles and trying to convince everyone here that I starve her, that she never gets any love and attention, and that she deserves to eat everything."

A wave of relief ran across Madison's face. She released a deep breath and then smiled. "It's the massage. It usually makes the dogs very relaxed and mellow." She laughed. "Plus, she had several hours of playtime and an oatmeal bath."

I stared at Aggie, whose eyes were half-closed. She looked about ready to take a nap. "She looks like she's drugged."

She laughed. "I assure you, she's just…chill."

"If you think Aggie's mellow, look at Turbo." David pointed to the Plott hound. He had stretched out on the rug and was asleep.

We were so engrossed in conversation we didn't notice Joe had come in.

He walked up and saw us watching Turbo sleep. "What have you done to my dog?"

We hesitated a moment and then everyone burst out laughing. It took some time for us to collect ourselves to share how much the massage relaxed his dog.

Joe walked over to Turbo. He had to shake the dog to wake him up. Turbo lifted his head and his tail wagged. He got up and stretched. Joe bent down to pet him. Turbo yawned and gave his face a lick.

When Joe stood up, he gave the dog a command to lie down. The dog obeyed immediately, but rather than the anxious excitement he normally showed, he slowly slid down.

Joe shook his head. "That's going to be the last massage you get."

Dr. Morgan arrived next. He, too, came bearing gifts. He brought a six-pack of beer. It was clear he'd picked it up at a nearby gas station, but it was the thought that mattered. I thanked him and escorted him outside.

Dixie's husband, Beau, came next. He brought Chyna and Leia, which was probably the only thing that could possibly motivate Aggie and Turbo to play. Outside, they engaged in a rousing game of chase.

Joe sat at the table drinking a beer, watching the dogs play.

"Feeling better?" I asked.

He nodded. "Actually, I do. Turbo is technically the property of the Lighthouse Dunes Police Department." He spoke slowly, with very little emotion, although I could tell by the look in his eyes, he felt very passionate about Turbo. "He's considered a tool, like a gun or a billy club. He's not supposed to socialize and play with other dogs."

I glanced up as Turbo played with Chyna, Leia, and Aggie.

"But he's a dog. He needs companionship and play." I struggled to find the right words to voice my objection. Eventually, I gave up. "That just seems cruel."

"I could be fired for that." He nodded toward the dogs. "But I refuse to treat him like…a tool. He's my partner. He risks his life every day. He deserves some fun."

I patted Joe's hand. I already liked him and was very glad that such a kind man cared about my daughter. My opinion of him went up several points.

"So what's the real reason we're here?" He took a sip of his beer. "What are you up to?"

I stared at him and tried to look shocked. I must have failed because he laughed.

Eventually, I gave up. "Is it that obvious?"

He shrugged. "Red thought you were up to something, the way you kept finding jobs for him."

Now I didn't have to fake the shock. It was genuine. "He never let on."

He grinned. "So what's up?"

"I know what I saw. I'm not crazy. I saw someone murdered and that someone looked a lot like Keri Lynn."

"What makes you think it was Dallas who did it?" He looked at me. "He's not the only male working there. If you didn't see the man's face, why couldn't it have been someone else?"

I thought about that. Why was I so sure the murderer was Dallas? "I don't know, but I just know it was him."

"Okay, so let's say Dallas did murder someone." He turned to face me. "We know it couldn't have been Keri Lynn. Who was it?"

"I think it was Heather. She was one of the staff that worked there." I explained how I'd met her the day I boarded Aggie and how much she looked like Keri Lynn.

We were intent on our conversation, and I hadn't noticed the others had joined us and were standing nearby listening until I heard a gasp. I turned in time to see Madison's face lose color.

"Oh. My. God."

David pulled out one of the chairs and helped her into a seat.

"I'm so sorry." I turned to David. "Get her something to drink."

He hurried over to the bar and came back with a glass of wine.

Madison took a sip.

I was glad to see some of the color start to return. I clasped her free hand. "I'm so sorry, dear."

She shook her head. "No, it's okay. I wasn't great friends with her." She took another sip of wine. "She didn't really socialize with the rest of us."

"Was she…" I looked for the right words.

"Was she having an affair with Dallas?" she asked.

I nodded. "It was just an impression. When she talked about him, she seemed very…familiar."

"Familiar is one way of putting it." She hesitated a moment. "We all knew there was something going on between the two of them. He tried to get it on with everyone, but the rest of us had too much self-respect to get involved with the boss, especially when his wife was right there."

"That must have taken a lot of…guts for them to have an affair with the wife right there."

Madison shrugged. "Maybe. Keri Lynn did a fair amount of flirting. She and the chef, Justin, seemed awfully cozy."

Monica Jill smacked her hand down on the table. "I told you there was something going on between those two."

We took napkins and wiped up the beverages that spilled from Monica Jill's enthusiastic outburst.

"He was totally and completely head over heels for Keri Lynn." Madison shrugged. "It's easy to see why. She was the real brains behind Pet Haven. She's the one who had the ideas and did all of the thinking. Dallas was the schmoozer. He met with bankers and golfed with the people he thought could help with their business."

"Did it bother him? The fling with Justin, or that his wife was the brains?" Joe asked.

Madison was silent for a moment and then shrugged. "He never acted like it bothered him. In fact…I think…I got the impression he liked it, at least the thinking part. It meant he didn't have to exert his own brain."

"Sounds like a louse," Beau said.

"Well, he is a bit of a louse." She shook her head. "I know this is going to sound crazy, but men fell in love with Keri Lynn. It was like she hypnotized them or something. They fell over themselves to make her happy, no matter what making her happy did to them. Dallas and Justin both adored Keri Lynn. I don't think there's anything they wouldn't have done for her."

"I wonder if 'anything' includes murder." I looked around the table, but no one had an answer.

"Dallas must not have been too head over heels if he was fooling around with one of his employees right under her nose," Monica Jill said. "That's rude and disrespectful."

"What's disrespectful?" B.J. flopped down on one of the chairs.

Beau immediately rose. "What can I get you to drink?"

She asked for a beer, and he hurried to get her one.

"Sorry I'm late." Red, clean and freshly shaven, came in.

I made introductions. Beau handed him a beer. Dixie handed him a grill apron we'd found at the grocery store. The apron was in camouflage with multiple pockets. We had stuffed the pockets with bottles of ketchup, mustard, a spray water bottle, and grill tools. There were six pockets that went diagonally across the top where we placed cans of beer and it came with an attached bottle opener. Across the top were the words Grill Sergeant.

Red laughed as he took the apron. He seemed slightly embarrassed by the attention, but he thanked us for the gift.

I decided to rescue him. "Okay now, we're all hungry so get busy."

He saluted and trotted over to the grill.

I went inside and got the meat, which had been marinating in the fridge, and brought it outside.

He thanked me again for the apron.

I handed him a platter with the steaks, burgers, kabobs, and chicken we'd arranged earlier. There were also several hot dogs, and he looked slightly surprised.

"What?"

"Nothing. I just wasn't expecting hot dogs. I didn't see buns in the kitchen. You may need to send Joe to the…"

I shook my head. "Those aren't for us."

He scowled. "Who are they for?"

I pointed. "Those are for the dogs." I started to walk away but stopped when I heard him mumbling.

"I can't believe I'm grilling hot dogs for dogs."

I turned quickly. "Did you say something?"

"Nope." He put the hot dogs on the grill. "Do you know how they want them cooked?"

"Well done." I stuck out my tongue. I heard him laughing as I walked up to the deck.

I went inside and brought out a tray of hors d'oeuvres and set it on one of the nearby tables we'd arranged to hold the food before I sat down.

B.J. was engaged in a passionate discussion with Dr. Morgan about whether or not a woman of average height and strength could have been the murderer.

"I'm just saying, based on my experience as a coroner, women are more likely to commit crimes from a distance." He turned to Joe. "Am I right, Officer?"

"Actually, he's right. Studies show ninety-nine percent of people who reported as having been strangled are women who were strangled by men, usually an intimate partner. Typically, women steer away from murders that rely on physical strength, like strangling." He held up a hand to forestall the objections he could see forming on B.J.'s lips. "I'm not saying women aren't strong or that they can't strangle a man or a woman. However, strangling someone with your bare hands takes a *lot* of strength. Not just to..." He looked around.

"Go ahead. We can take it, blue eyes." B.J. took a swig from her beer, then leaned forward and batted her eyelashes at him playfully.

Joe looked around the table at the other women. Each one nodded. He took a breath. "It's not just the strength needed to constrict the airflow to the brain or cause damage to the larynx or damage the..."

Dr. Morgan intervened. "Hyoid or other bones in the neck."

Joe nodded. "It's not just that, but being attacked releases endorphins. Unless the person has been drugged first to help subdue them, they'll thrash about. They'll claw and struggle and flop around."

"The sensation...we call air hunger...is so terrifying, it can actually induce violent struggling." Dr. Morgan shook his head. "It's pretty horrible." He took a sip of beer.

Joe continued, "In my opinion, unless a garrote of some type is used, strangulation is a form of dominance. It's not just a way to murder someone. The killer is making a statement."

"What kind of statement?" I asked.

"He's saying, 'I'm dominant. I have control over you. I control the very air you breathe.'" His voice was soft. "We see it a lot with domestic violence cases."

We sat quietly for several minutes.

B.J. sat up. "Well, that's a buzzkill."

After a long pause, everyone laughed and the mood of heaviness lifted.

Monica Jill leaned forward. "Okay, so you think Dallas killed Heather and Keri Lynn."

I nodded.

She glanced at Red. "The police don't believe you?"

"It's not that…I mean, the police need proof, and we don't have anything except my word to go on."

Monica Jill, Dixie, B.J., and Dr. Morgan all exchanged glances.

Whether by general consent or personality, Monica Jill acted as spokesperson. "That's good enough for us." She glanced at each of them again, and they all nodded in turn. "What do you need us to do?"

I looked at my new friends and was overwhelmed by emotion. These people barely knew me, yet they listened to me and trusted me. I blinked back tears. "Thank you."

B.J. took a swig of her beer. "Do we get to wear tight black leather pants and cool black T-shirts?" She flipped her head back as though flipping her hair out of her face and then hopped up from her seat and struck a pose I recognized from the *Charlie's Angels* posters. "I think I should be Lucy Liu."

Unfortunately, Joe had just taken a sip of his beer and barely avoided spraying it all over Dr. Morgan. Instead, he spit it out over the deck rail and everyone laughed.

Eventually, Monica Jill gave B.J.'s butt a playful swat. "Will you sit your hiney down so we can find out what we need to do?"

When I was able to talk without laughing, I turned to B.J. "Did you say you live in the same subdivision as Dallas and Keri Lynn?"

B.J. nodded. "Yep. My house isn't as *grand* as theirs, but I figure they're bringing my property values up with that ten-thousand-square-foot monstrosity."

"Ten thousand?" I nearly choked.

She nodded. "You bet. I snuck in when they were having it built and it's ginormous." She smiled. "So I sold them a fantastic rate on insurance if they bundled their home, auto, and the business." She shook her head. "That was one of the biggest insurance policies I ever wrote. It's not often you get to write a policy on a Tesla."

"Tesla." Joe sat up. "He has a Tesla?"

She shook her head. "Keri Lynn has a Tesla. Dallas has a lowly BMW."

Based on the look of admiration that crossed the faces of David, Joe, Dr. Morgan, and Beau, I knew there must be something amazing about the Tesla. "What's so special about that?" I asked.

You would have thought I'd asked if the earth was flat based on the looks I got. I glanced at Dixie, who merely shrugged.

David leaned forward in his seat. "Mom, you don't know what a Tesla is?"

"I'm assuming it's a car. It's also the name of a famous inventor." I shrugged. "What's the big deal?"

I could tell by the look in my son's eyes, I'd lost whatever cool mom points I had previously.

"Tesla is the name of a car manufacturer. They make energy-efficient electric cars." Dixie read from her cell phone.

David shook his head. "It's not just an electric car. It's the most amazingly spectacular car ever." His eyes glistened, and his face radiated as he extolled the virtues of the car.

Monica Jill snapped her fingers. "Didn't I read something in the news about those cars? They drive themselves."

David nodded. "They have a self-driving car." He looked like an excited kid. "You don't have to do anything. You just get in the car and tell it where you want to go and it takes you there." He threw his hands up in the air. "That's so cool."

I frowned. "Sounds dangerous to me."

He dropped his head on the table.

"Sounds expensive to me," Dixie said.

"It's expensive." B.J. nodded. "They start at a hundred grand."

I whistled.

"Mr. Simpson used to brag about how much the car cost and how he got it specially modified for Keri Lynn because she was left-handed." Madison sipped her wine.

"The article I saw in the news was about one of those self-driving cars that crashed." Monica Jill glanced around the table.

I turned to Joe. "Do you think Keri Lynn's crash could have had something to do with the self-driving feature of her car?"

He shrugged. "I doubt it."

Beau had been very quiet, but he looked up. "I play golf with the guy who owns the Tesla dealership. I could probably ask a few questions."

I looked at him. "That would be great. Maybe he could tell you when it was serviced last." I paused for several moments to collect my thoughts. "Also, I would imagine a car that drives itself would have a lot of technology."

He nodded.

"Maybe there's some way to download that technology to see what happened."

Beau nodded. "I'll see what I can find out."

I thought for a few moments. "Dallas and Keri Lynn have fancy cars and a big house."

"I'm still stuck back on ten thousand square feet," Dixie said. "Do they have kids?"

B.J. shook her head. "Nope. It's just the two of them. But what's really weird is you'd expect them to have dogs. I mean, they own a pet resort, but they don't have dogs."

We all agreed that was definitely weird.

Dr. Morgan whistled. "I guess the pet resort business must be doing pretty well if they can afford a huge house like that."

"Hmm…must not be doing too well." B.J. took a sip of her beer. "Today I noticed there's a For Sale sign in the yard."

We were shocked. "Really? I wonder why they're selling." I stared at Monica Jill.

"I'm sure I can find out. The real estate community is pretty small."

I nodded. "Great. Use your contacts and see what you can find out about why they're selling."

I looked at B.J. "You take Snowball to Pet Haven, right?"

"Snowball is scheduled for a mani-pedi," B.J. responded.

I stared at her. "You've got to be joking?"

She smiled. "I'm terrible at clipping her nails. I cut the quick once and it took forever to stop the bleeding. Now she runs and hides when she sees me with a pair of nail clippers." She sighed. "Anyway, it's what they call it when they clip her nails. It sounds a lot more impressive than it really is."

I shook my head. "Could you talk to the person who does her grooming and find out if they've heard anything about Heather and Dallas or Justin and Keri Lynn. Boy, he must be pretty broken up." I stared at Madison.

"You should have seen him. He actually howled." She shivered.

David nodded. "It was awful."

I turned to B.J. "You're going to need to be…subtle. You don't want them to catch on."

She twisted her lips. "I've got this. I can be subtle when I want to be." She smiled. "My money is on Justin. I think he did her in. I'm going to talk to some folks and see what I can find out."

I turned to Dr. Morgan. "How many coroners are there in the city?"

He smiled. "One."

"So you'll be performing the autopsy on Keri Lynn?"

He nodded. "Anything in particular you want me to look for?"

I glanced at Joe.

"Do you have a mass spectrometer?" Joe asked.

"I wish." Dr. Morgan shook his head. "However, I have a friend in Nashville."

"What's a mass spectro—" Dixie asked.

B.J. bounced in her chair. "I know. They use that all the time on *NCIS*. It's this huge machine that can analyze stuff for different chemicals. Abby uses it all the time."

I looked to Dr. Morgan, who merely shrugged. "Basically, she's right. It ionizes chemical samples by using—"

I held up a hand to stop the flow of words. "So it can tell if she was poisoned or drugged?"

Dr. Morgan nodded.

"Look for punctures and run a full toxicology report," Joe added.

Dr. Morgan nodded.

"What about me?" Madison asked.

"Well..." I looked at David.

"Are you sure you're up to it?" he asked.

She nodded. "I want to help too. After all, I knew Keri Lynn and Heather better than anyone else here. Keri Lynn was my boss. If she was murdered, I want to help put her killer behind bars."

"Well, I don't want to draw attention to you, but...well, the story Dallas spread around is that Heather had a family emergency. When you started, did you have to list an emergency contact?"

She nodded.

"It would be really helpful if you could check her employee file and find out her address and the name of her emergency contact."

She looked pale, and her gaze darted around.

"If you're not up to it—"

"No. No. I'll be fine. I can do it."

I stared at David.

He smiled. "Don't worry. I'll watch out for her."

I looked around. "I think that's everybody."

"What about me?" Dixie asked.

I smiled. "I have a special assignment for you that will be right up your alley."

Before she could ask further questions, Red came up the stairs with the food.

"Dinner is ready!"

The food was delicious, and everyone seemed to genuinely enjoy themselves. We sat outside and ate, laughed, and drank.

Joe was the first to leave. He stretched. "I've got to hit the road early tomorrow."

I hugged him. "I wish you weren't leaving so soon."

"Thank you, but I'm sure Stephanie and I will be back. She was so disappointed she couldn't come along this time."

Turbo stretched and yawned several times but eventually he followed Joe to the car.

Red was the last to leave. He cleaned the grill and helped me load the dishes into the dishwasher, put away the extra food, and get the house tidy. When we were done, I walked him to the door.

He looked into my eyes. "Look, I know you haven't given up investigating."

I started to talk, but he held up a hand to stop me.

"I also know there's nothing I can do to stop you. You're an adult, and you're going to do whatever you want to do anyway."

I smiled.

"However, you can't stop me from worrying. I've seen too many murders, and I don't want you to get hurt."

He took a finger and traced it down the side of my face, and I had to work hard to focus on what he was saying. "I may not be able to help with the investigation from an official standpoint, but I can try to keep an eye on you and work on things unofficially."

"I appreciate that, but I don't want you to get in any more trouble because of me."

He held me. "Trouble is my middle name."

We lingered over our good-byes until Aggie prompted us to move things along by standing on her hind legs and pushing Red in the back of his knees.

He laughed. "Okay, I'm leaving." He gave Aggie a pat and left.

Aggie yawned and stretched.

"Okay, you're very pushy when you're tired." I made sure all of the doors were locked and headed to bed. Aggie followed me until she saw I was finally heading to bed and then rushed to the bedroom, climbed the stairs I'd bought to allow her to get into my bed, and then plopped down on my pillow.

I let her stay until I finished my nightly routine and then shifted her over to her side of the bed.

Aggie was snoring before I got the lights out. However, sleep eluded me. I tossed and turned. I repositioned my pillow, tried sleeping with covers off and then covers on, but nothing worked. Eventually, Aggie must have gotten tired of my tossing and got off the bed and went into her dog bed in the crate I kept near the side of the bed.

I sat up and turned on the light. "Traitor."

Aggie's eyes fluttered, she stood up and turned in a circle, and finally settled down with her back to me.

I pulled out the notepad and pen I kept beside my bed and tried to make sense of everything. Why would Dallas murder both his wife and his girlfriend? I could easily come up with a motive for killing one or the other of them, but both…why? I tapped the pen. "I must be wrong. This doesn't make any sense."

I stared across at Aggie, but she ignored my late-night musings.

I flipped the page in my notebook. I wrote the Sherlock Holmes quote across the top. *Once you eliminate the impossible, whatever remains, no matter how improbable, must be the truth.*

What was impossible? I thought about it and then wrote: *It was impossible for Dallas Simpson to have killed the same woman twice.* If he murdered Keri Lynn last Sunday, then she couldn't have been in a gas station in Georgia today. He might have tampered with—her brakes or something underneath the car that could have caused an accident, but he certainly couldn't have dressed up her dead body and manipulated it like a puppet. Or could he?

I was deeply engrossed in my notebook when Aggie sat up, growled, and then ran across the room barking. I sat very still and concentrated, cell phone in hand. I pressed 911 but stopped before pressing the button to initiate the call and listened. The barking stopped. After a few moments, there was a knock on the door, and I recognized David's voice.

"Mom, are you up?"

"Come in." I put my cell phone back down on the nightstand.

David stuck his head inside. He had a sheepish grin on his face and a black poodle on his chest. "Don't tell me you're waiting up."

"To be completely honest, I forgot you were out, dear. How is Madison? Is she still shaky?"

David came in and sat on the bed. "She's better. I think the party helped. Thanks for inviting her."

"Of course. She's a nice girl."

He petted Aggie, but his mind seemed miles away. Eventually, he looked up. "Nice. Yeah, she is nice." He stroked Aggie.

I got the impression he wanted to say more, so I waited.

He sat for several moments.

"Was there something you wanted to say?"

"Hmm…no." He put Aggie down. "No, I just wondered what you thought of her, that's all."

"I don't really know her, but she's very pretty and she has nice manners." I shrugged. "I've really only known her a couple of days, so I don't have much to base an opinion on."

He nodded. "I guess when it boils down to it, I've only known her a couple of days too. Although it feels like we've known each other a lot longer."

"Well, you've spent a lot more time with her than I have." I patted his leg. "I do like her. I just don't know her, that's all."

"Well, I'll have to see what I can do about that." He headed for the door.

"I hope that means I'm going to see a lot more of you."

He smiled and blew me a kiss.

My brain had started to land on an idea, but it was gone now. I knew enough to realize that forcing it wouldn't help, so I gave up and went to sleep. This time I was successful—I wrestled the elusive Sandman to the ground and snatched several hours of sleep.

Sunday, I awoke to the smell of coffee. I got up and picked up a still-snoozing Aggie. She wasn't thrilled with being awakened, but I wouldn't be thrilled when I came out of the shower if she'd left me a few surprises either. So I went to the back and put her outside.

David was sitting at the dining room table sending text messages. His brow was furrowed, and his lips were set in a straight line.

We grunted greetings while I brewed a cup of coffee. By the time the coffee finished, I opened the back door and let Aggie in.

I drank the coffee on my way to my room. I showered, dressed, and got ready for mass.

I waved to David and walked out to the car.

Mass in Chattanooga was much the same as mass in Indiana, although the people in the South were definitely a lot friendlier, less inhibited, and noisier than those in the North. One woman in particular seemed to lack the inhibitions that plagued a lot of Roman Catholics. Instead of the conservative, pious attitude that could be taken as snooty, she was very free in her worship. She raised her hands during the service. She swayed when singing and often yelled "Amen" or "Praise the Lord" when the priest was speaking. Her face radiated with a joy that made me smile at her enthusiasm. One of the other members must have noticed me glancing in her direction and shared that the woman had been Pentecostal but converted to Catholicism when she got married, as though that explained everything. I merely smiled and nodded as though I understood.

When I got home, David was dressed but still sat in the same spot at the table. I changed out of my Sunday clothes and joined him in the kitchen.

He stared into space. After a few moments, he must have made a decision. He sat up, leaned forward, and looked at me. "Mom, there's something I want to talk to you about."

His tone was so serious that immediately my heart rate increased. I took several deep breaths and braced myself. "Okay, sure."

"It's about Madison."

It had been quite some time since he'd talked to me about girls, but considering he'd only known her for a few days, I couldn't imagine anything too serious and allowed myself to relax. "What about her?"

"There's something...in her past...that well, I don't even know if I should be telling you this. I mean you wouldn't tell Joe or Red, right?"

I frowned. "That depends. I mean, if she was involved in something illegal..."

He shook his head. "No, she's not...I mean, not anymore...I mean."

I clasped his hands. "David, just tell me what it is."

He nodded. "She's really smart." He smiled. "She's a computer nerd."

"Okay." I paused. "That's not a crime."

"Not unless you get into hacking information."

My eyes got big, and after a few seconds, I realized my mouth was open and closed it. "You're telling me Madison is a computer hacker."

"Not anymore. She was a hacker, but she told me she hasn't done any hacking in years."

I nodded slowly. "Well, that's good. What did she hack?"

He took a deep breath. "The way I understand it, there are basically three types of hackers. White Hat, Black Hat, and Gray Hat. White Hat Hackers are hired by companies to identify gaps in security. They break into systems with permission. They aren't trying to use the information for their own personal gain."

I nodded. "Okay. So, I assume the Black Hat Hackers are the bad guys who break into systems to get information without permission and they use the information for their personal gain."

He nodded.

"So, what do the Gray Hat Hackers do?"

"They break into systems, without permission, but they aren't trying to use the information they find for their own personal gain. Usually, they notify the company they infiltrated about the breach and may be hired to fix it...for a fee."

"What type of hacker is Madison?"

"Gray Hat." He glanced at me and quickly added, "But she doesn't do that anymore."

"I take it she got caught?"

He nodded. "She was young, and the judge gave her probation and community service. That's how she got into dogs. Her community service work was with a no-kill animal shelter."

"So, how did she end up at Pet Haven?"

"She needed a paying job." He looked up. "She still volunteers at the shelter."

I patted his hand. "That's great, but why are you telling me this?"

"She was worried you or Red would find out and might think that because she has a record…"

I nodded. "We might think she might be guilty of other crimes like murder?"

"Yeah."

"Well, I don't think she murdered Keri Lynn or Heather, and I stand by my initial assessment."

He looked puzzled.

"She seems like a nice girl."

He beamed. "She is nice." He got serious. "She says she can tap in to Dallas and Keri Lynn's systems if you want her to…if it would help."

I took a minute to think, but then shook my head. "No. I don't want to encourage her to break the law. Although I suppose asking her to get Heather's address is straddling the fence between Black Hat and White Hat." I paused.

He smiled and reached into a pocket and pulled out a piece of paper. "She got that in less than five minutes."

I opened the paper. There was an address, which I assumed was Heather's. I glanced at David.

"She said there was no emergency contact listed."

"Please thank her for me, but no more hacking."

He reached across and kissed me on the cheek. "I'm starving. What's for lunch?"

Chapter 15

The remainder of Sunday was uneventful. David and I had lunch and then I took him to the airport, where he reserved a rental car. I suspected he wanted wheels of his own so he and Madison could spend time together, and that was perfectly okay with me. Afterward, he left to spend the day with Madison, while Aggie and I explored our new neighborhood. There wasn't much to explore from my standpoint, but Aggie took her sweet time sniffing and marking along the way. I took the opportunity during the walk to try to get things ordered in my mind. I felt confident Dallas Simpson was guilty. However, I couldn't figure out why. Eventually, I gave up trying and decided to allow my mind to wander where it would as I enjoyed the walk with Aggie.

When we got home, Red called and offered to cook dinner. I loved dating a man who enjoyed cooking. Although I would need to exercise more if I continued to eat his delicious Southern cuisine.

On the menu tonight was meat loaf, mashed potatoes, and turnip greens. I'll admit, prior to coming to Tennessee, I had never tried turnip greens. Now I was addicted to them. We sat on the deck afterward and enjoyed the weather.

"What time did Joe leave this morning?"

Red sipped his wine. "Five. He wanted to get home and rest before it got late."

"I hope Turbo is recovered from his massage."

He smiled. "He certainly slept well. That dog snored so loud I could hear him in my bedroom."

I chuckled. "He works hard and deserved a break. I hope it won't prevent him from doing his police work."

"I'm sure he'll be back to work first thing tomorrow."

We sat in a companionable silence for several minutes.

Red broke the silence. "Did you get your sleuths on the right track?"

"What do you mean?"

"Come on. I know what you were up to last night." He worked to hide a smile. "You haven't given up on this."

I should have known I couldn't hide what I was doing from a trained investigator. "I haven't given up. I know what I saw."

"And no amount of evidence will convince you that maybe you were mistaken?"

I shook my head. "What evidence?"

Red pulled his cell phone out of his pocket. "I shouldn't be showing this to you." He glanced at me but continued to swipe his cell phone. Eventually, he pulled up what he was looking for and pressed Play.

On the screen was a grainy image of a gas station in black and white. A tall, thin woman got out of her car, swiped her credit card, and filled her tank. When she was done, she went inside and purchased a Diet Coke. Even though the image wasn't the highest quality and I had only met her once, I knew the woman in the image was Keri Lynn Simpson.

When the video was done, Red stared in my eyes. "Well?"

"It's her. That's Keri Lynn."

He nodded. "So are you ready to let this drop?"

I shook my head. "I know it doesn't make any sense. I'm not sure how he did it, but I know what I saw."

He sighed and shook his head. "What will it take to convince you?"

I thought about it. What would it take to convince me I didn't see Keri Lynn murdered? "Medical records, DNA."

He shook his head. "Your friend in the coroner's office is working on that. In the meantime, let's not talk about DNA or evidence or anything else connected to Keri Lynn or Pet Haven."

We spent the remainder of the afternoon talking about the house. Once the loan was final and I could close on the house, I had big plans for remodeling the master bathroom and the kitchen. Money permitting, I planned to also screen in a section of the back deck. Since moving to the South, I had become enamored with screened-in porches. The weather was so mild, I would be able to use the porch year-round, even when the winters were normal temperatures instead of the unseasonably warm weather we were having now.

Later, when Red left and I was home alone, I pondered what he'd said. Could I have been wrong? The video didn't lie. It was definitely Keri Lynn at that gas station. Unless the murder was staged, I don't know how I could be mistaken. I forced myself to remember and relive what I'd seen a week prior. Was it only one week since I saw a human being lose her life? I didn't want to face the truth of what I'd seen, but I had to. So I braced myself both mentally and physically. I wasn't sure why hanging on to the edge of the mattress helped, but for some reason, it did. I took a deep breath and allowed my mind to wander. Just when the mental image popped into my mind, my cell phone rang.

I looked at the picture.

It was Stephanie. "Hi, Mom. You busy?"

"Hello, dear. Not especially."

We chatted for several moments about nothing, but then she came to the heart of the matter. "I wanted to let you know Joe made it back to Lighthouse Dunes safely."

I was glad for the update.

Before she got off the phone, she said, "I was fiddling around on the computer, and I ran across something odd about that woman you saw murdered."

I sat up in bed. She had my full attention now.

"It's not anything sinister, just odd. So when her first husband died, there was an investigation into the death, because he had taken out a big life insurance policy about six months before he died."

"How big?"

"One million dollars."

I whistled. "That's big. Did the insurance company pay? Did they think there was something wrong?"

Stephanie laughed. "Mom, don't get excited. The insurance company filed for an investigation into the death." She must have sensed I was preparing to interrupt because she hurried on. "It's common for an insurance company to investigate if a large insurance policy is taken out and then the person dies. However, the result of the investigation was that it was a tragic accident. Keri Lynn was three hours away at the time of the crash, and there was no evidence of foul play."

"Oh." I sighed.

Stephanie chuckled. "Only you would be disappointed that someone wasn't actually murdered. I just thought it was strange."

We agreed it was strange, but neither of us could come up with a good reason why it mattered. So we chatted a bit longer before we got off the phone. I pondered the insurance angle, but considering Keri Lynn had been more than three hours away and the cause of death was natural causes, I didn't see how this factored in. However, I made a mental note to ask B.J. about it.

Monday, I struggled to get back into the swing of getting up and going to work, but I forced myself. I got up and dressed and let Aggie out to take care of her business. I was glad she would be home with David and wouldn't have to be crated while I was out. So, once she came inside, I opened the guest bedroom door wide enough for her to slip through and quickly closed it. I waited until I heard David grumbling and then hurried off.

Linda Kay's office door was open, and I could hear snatches of conversation as I approached. When I got to the executive director's door, I stuck my head inside. "What's going on?"

"I'm trying to convince Jacob we don't need him and he needs to go home." Linda Kay rolled her scooter to the large conference table that took up one side of her vast office.

Jacob sat at the table, which was set with coffee, tea, china, and a box from Da Vinci's. "And I've been trying to convince Mrs. Weyman that I'm perfectly capable of returning to work." Jacob poured a cup of coffee into a china cup and took a sip.

"Are those scones?" I sniffed the air like a rabbit.

Jacob smiled. "These aren't just any ol' scones, these are Da Vinci's famous lemon scones with vanilla lemon glaze." He glanced at me over his teacup. "And they're still warm. You better hurry."

"Let me put my purse away." I hurried next door to my office, which was smaller than Linda Kay's but still as grand. Jacob must have arrived very early because my door was unlocked and the blinds were open just the way I liked. There was also a crystal vase of flowers on my desk, which were my favorites, Asiatic lilies. I took a quick sniff and then hurried next door.

I sat down and took a bite of a warm lemon scone and allowed the vanilla lemon glaze to melt in my mouth. I worked hard to keep a moan from escaping; at least I thought I did. However, when I opened my eyes, both Linda Kay and Jacob were looking at me.

"Do you need a moment alone with that?" Jacob joked.

Linda Kay laughed, but I didn't really care.

We ate in silence for several moments.

After my second scone, and I think my third cup of coffee, I turned to Jacob. "You must have gotten here pretty early to have done all of this." I spread my hands out to encompass the entire table. "And thank you for the flowers."

Linda Kay ate the crumbs from a raspberry chocolate tart. "Yes, thank you for the flowers."

I glanced at her desk and saw she also had a vase of flowers, although hers were yellow roses in a blue and white Chinese vase. If I remembered correctly, it was a Ming Dynasty vase from Linda Kay's personal collection, which was worth a small fortune. However, she believed items were to be used as the artist intended rather than to be placed behind glass and merely admired. Unusual attitude for someone who worked at a museum, but it was one of the things I loved about her.

"You're both very welcome." Jacob held up a hand. "Before you both start in on me again"—he reached inside his breast pocket and flourished a small piece of paper, which he passed over to Linda Kay—"a note from my doctor saying I am able to return to work."

Linda Kay opened the note and read. When she was finished, she folded the note and held it up. "How do I know this isn't a forgery?" Her lips twitched.

Jacob feigned shock. "*Moi?* I can't believe you think I'd do something so…low and common as to forge a doctor's note. I'm hurt that you believe me capable of deceiving you…after all these years." He sniffed and took a napkin and dabbed at his eyes.

"It's because of all of our years together that I know what you're capable of." She turned to me. "Lilly?"

"I might not have worked with you for *years*, but I firmly believe you capable of not only forging your doctor's signature but, after visiting you at your mother's house, I feel pretty confident—"

"Alright." Jacob picked up the note and tore it to shreds. "I did forge the note." He flung the pieces in the air. Then he grinned. "However, I have been cleared to return to work, part-time." He reached inside another pocket and pulled out a different note.

Linda Kay glanced at the note. "It says you have restrictions." She looked around. "Where are your crutches?"

He rolled his eyes and then reached under the table and pulled out a crutch. "I haven't mastered this thing yet, and frankly, I find it more trouble than it's worth."

"Well, if you want to work, you better master that thing, and don't let me see you without it." She shook a playful finger at him.

Jacob sat up straight and saluted. "Ay, ay, Captain."

Linda Kay laughed. "Stop it."

We listened to Jacob's experiences. After a few minutes, he announced that Linda Kay would need to hustle if she intended to make her board meeting.

I stood and started to clean up the table but was stopped when Jacob announced he was fully capable of cleaning up a few plates and ordered me out of the room. I started to protest but was interrupted by a tap on the door.

I turned and saw a young girl I'd noticed working downstairs in the museum's cafeteria, whom I suspected had a serious crush on Jacob, standing at the door.

"Excuse me, but are you ready for me to clear up?"

Jacob nodded.

The young girl rolled a cart in the room and loaded the dishes onto the cart.

"Lilly, this is Emily."

She nodded and smiled.

"Emily works downstairs and has graciously agreed to help me out." He smiled at Emily, who blushed and continued loading the tea items onto the cart with her head down. "It turns out she lives close to my mom's, so she was able to drive me to work." He pointed to the compression boot. "Which is a godsend, because this boot makes it virtually impossible to drive a stick shift."

In that moment, I had a flash. In that instant, I knew why the video about Keri Lynn at the gas station bothered me. I hurried to my office and left the two of them to clean up alone.

Back in my office, I called Red but couldn't reach him. Instead, I left him a message that I had something I wanted to tell him. I asked if he was free for lunch and told him to please bring the video of Keri Lynn and any crime scene photos of the accident.

After a few moments, he sent a text saying he'd pick me up for lunch.

I forced my brain to think on other things. It took a bit, but eventually I allowed my mind to focus on accounting. I quickly lost myself in figures. The museum's books had been in bad shape when I started, but I took great pride in knowing things were straightened out to the point that I almost longed for an IRS audit—almost. I imagined a blue-suited bean counter gushing about my balance sheets and financial statements. Perhaps the IRS would even provide me with an award for my services to the accounting world. I was jolted out of my fantasy when my cell phone rang.

I looked at the phone and saw Red's picture. "Good morning."

"Good afternoon."

I looked at the time. "I stand corrected."

"I'm downtown. I can pick you up in ten minutes."

Something in the tone of his voice let me know he was in an exceptionally good mood. "You sound happy. What's going on?"

He chuckled. "Maybe I'm just happy to know I get to see you."

Heat rose up my neck. "As much as I'd like to believe that, I'm guessing you got some good news."

"I'll explain when I see you." He rang off.

I had just enough time to check my makeup and grab my purse. By the time I got downstairs, Red was walking around to open my car door.

Once I was in, he hurried around to get in the car, and I couldn't help but notice a certain amount of pep in his step.

He drove to a small barbecue restaurant we'd found while exploring the city. The food was good, but the owners were the real attraction. An African American man whom everyone called Moose and his wife, Renee. When we arrived, Moose greeted us as he always did, with a big smile.

He brought us menus, and he and Red talked football. Moose was a popular football player in college and had even played in the NFL for a year until he blew out his knees. He and Renee met in college but drifted apart. Both got married and started families. Renee had been happily married for over thirty years until her husband died unexpectedly. Moose had been unhappily married for the same amount of time. When he finally, in his words, "got sick and tired of being sick and tired," he applied for a divorce. He and Renee reconnected at a class reunion. They got married and opened their restaurant so Moose could do what he liked, smoke barbecue. The two men talked football until Renee came over and told Moose to stop bothering us and to get back to the kitchen. Renee was a light-skinned woman with a short Afro. The food was good, but the entertainment came from watching the two of them interact. They were obviously in love, and it warmed my heart to see how they interacted with each other and bantered back and forth.

After we placed our orders, Renee left and promised to keep her husband away so we could enjoy our meals in peace. She gave me a wink and then hurried to take care of other customers.

"Did you bring the video?"

Red reached in his pocket and pulled out his cell phone. He swiped the screen until he got where he wanted and then passed it across the table to me.

I pressed Play and we watched Keri Lynn get out of a white BMW SUV. That was when I paused the video. "See, it's the wrong car."

He stared at the screen. "What are you talking about?"

"Remember, Keri Lynn doesn't have a BMW. She has a Tesla." I watched the light bulb go off and his eyes light up. "Madison said Dallas talked about how much he spent customizing the Tesla for Keri Lynn because she was left-handed."

Unfortunately, the light bulb went out far too quickly. "Okay, so why is that important?"

I hadn't really thought about that, but I wasn't ready to give up quite so easily. "Well, it proves that Keri Lynn was driving Dallas's car. He could have easily tampered with the brakes or some other thing underneath the car so the car would careen down a mountain and explode."

"Maybe he had to take her car in for service."

I refused to allow Red to dampen my spirits. "I'll know soon enough. Beau knows the Tesla dealer, and he's going to ask when the car was last serviced."

He nodded.

"So, what has you in such a good mood today?" I sipped my lemon water and gazed over the top of my glass at Red.

He reached in his pocket and pulled out an envelope.

I reached across, but he hesitated. "I'm not sure I should show you this. It's photos from the crime scene. There's no body, but the car is in really bad shape."

I took a deep breath and reached across for the photos. The white car was mangled and scorched and barely looked like anything more than scrap metal. I flipped the photos slowly and then flipped through them again. Something flashed across my mind. However, it left as quickly as it came. So I went through the photos again, this time more slowly. "Why would the photos of a burned-out car make you excited?"

"Because your friend from the dog club, Dr. Morgan, has declared the accident to be suspicious."

I looked up. "Really? Because of these photos?"

He nodded. "Well, partly because of the photos." He glanced at me. "Plus, there are some weird things going on with the body." He hesitated.

"Give it to me."

He shrugged. "The body was pretty badly burned. However, he did find some things that puzzled him."

I patted the table impatiently. "Spill it."

He looked around. "He had someone drive the tissue and blood samples to Nashville, and apparently there was some evidence that the body had been drugged."

Renee brought our food and plenty of napkins. We threw etiquette and silverware to the wind and picked up our ribs with our hands and sucked the barbecue sauce off of our fingers while we talked. The napkins were to protect our clothes from splatters.

"Are you sure you want to hear this?" Red asked. "It's not exactly mealtime conversation."

I nodded. "Spill it."

He shrugged. "The body was burned really badly…too badly. He thinks an accelerant was used. Although if it's gasoline, then it could have been from the accident. She could have spilled gas on her shoes or stepped in a spill when she was filling her tank. However, the teeth are missing."

"Her teeth?" I shook my head. "Could that have happened from the car accident? Maybe she hit her head on the steering wheel or if the air bag deployed. I've heard those can cause a lot of damage."

"It could. However, without teeth it makes it really hard to identify the victim. Plus, she doesn't have any family members we can use to help with identification. So, no teeth and a badly burned body, and when you combine that with the fact he found evidence of frostbite on the victim's feet…"

I stopped with corn on the cob midway to my mouth. "Frostbite?"

He nodded.

"How does a woman killed in a car fire get frostbite?"

"Exactly."

I stared at him. "Does this mean what I think it means?"

He nodded. "If you're thinking suspicious death, then the answer is yes."

"Does this mean they believe you?"

He nodded. "It means I'm no longer on suspension and we are investigating the case as a possible homicide."

Chapter 16

The remainder of my day went quickly. At five, Dixie met me downtown. As a native, she knew her way around Chattanooga and was able to find Heather's address easily.

As it turned out, the address she took me to was relatively close to Jacob's mother's home in Red Bank.

We pulled up in front of a small bungalow.

"What's our story?" Dixie peered out of the passenger window.

"I'm just going to say I was concerned. I heard about the family emergency and wanted to make sure she was okay." I stared at Dixie. "I should have brought flowers."

She reached to the back seat. "How about a bottle of wine?" She held up a bottle of moscato.

"You come prepared, don't you?" I opened the door.

"Just like the Boy Scouts." She got out of the car and walked around to the sidewalk.

We walked up to the front door. It was a small house in a quiet neighborhood of equally small houses. The grass was overgrown, and there was a week's worth of papers on the front porch.

We rang the doorbell and waited. When no one answered, we rang it again and followed that up with a knock.

"Ain't nobody home."

We looked around to see who was talking.

A short, older woman with an extremely high-pitched voice and a large red wig like the one Dustin Hoffman wore in *Tootsie* yelled from the porch next door. "Ain't nobody home."

Dixie smiled big and walked across the yard. "Hi. My name is Dixie, and this is my friend, Lilly Ann. We're looking for Heather. Do you know when she'll be back?"

The woman sat on a kitchen chair. "My name's Clara. Everyone around here calls me Miss Clara," she announced in her squeaky voice.

"Hello, Miss Clara. We heard Heather had a family emergency, and we were worried about her," Dixie said.

The old woman pulled her cotton housecoat closer. "I don't know nothing 'bout no family emergency. Don't seem possible, seeing as she ain't got no family to speak of." She chewed and then leaned over and spit a brown wad of spittle into a Folgers coffee can.

I recoiled and tried to adjust my face not to show my surprise. Eventually, I pulled myself together. "She told me she was raised by her grandmother."

Miss Clara nodded. "Yep, that would be Adelaide...Adelaide Morgan." She shook her head. "No finer woman on this earth than Adelaide Morgan." Her eyes filled with tears. "Been gone five years now."

"I'm so sorry. Were you good friends?" Dixie asked.

Miss Clara nodded and used her sleeve to wipe her eyes. "Sure was. Me and Adelaide go way back." She turned and spit again. "I remember when little Heather came to live with her." She leaned close. "Mother got on the bottle and the state took Heather away. Brought her here when she was knee-high to a grasshopper."

"So, Adelaide raised her?" I asked.

"Yep. Sure did. Fine young girl she turned out to be too." Miss Clara held her back straight and sat up tall.

"Do you have any idea where she could have gone?" I asked.

Miss Clara shook her head. "Nope. Ain't seen her for going on a week now. Which is pretty odd, now I come to think on it. Ain't seen that there dog of hers either."

I asked a few more questions, but there wasn't really anything more Miss Clara could add. Dixie made a friend for life when she offered Miss Clara the bottle of wine.

Dixie took me back to the museum for my car, and we promised to touch base tomorrow after obedience class.

David had left a note that he and Aggie were out with Madison. So I was home alone for the first time since I'd moved in. The house was quiet. I thought about calling Red, but I decided not to. I was a big girl. If I was going to buy this house, then I would need to get accustomed to living here alone. Sitting on the back deck, I sipped a glass of wine and relaxed. I listened to the wind and the birds and tried to listen to my subconscious.

Unfortunately, my subconscious didn't have much to say. I must have dozed off because the next thing I remember was David shaking me and telling me I'd catch cold if I stayed outside all night.

Aggie walked past me and took care of her business. When she went inside, she surprised both David and me by passing my bedroom and walking into the guest bedroom.

I stared at David, who merely shrugged and followed her to bed.

Tuesday was a busy day at work, but unlike most nights when I had obedience class, tonight was a lot easier. Thanks to the fact David was visiting, I wouldn't have to rush home, change clothes, grab Aggie, and then head to the ETDC building. Tonight, David took Aggie to Pet Haven to pick up Madison. They would meet us at the club.

I brought an extra pair of clothes to work to change into, so I had an hour alone to make it to class. I barely knew what to do with myself. I decided to grab a snack, although I didn't want to eat too much because we were going to have pizza after training tonight and discuss what we'd found out.

Everyone was at training on time and there was a buzz of excitement as everyone talked about what they'd learned. However, Dixie put a stop to it when she entered with Chyna and Leia and started in on our lesson.

Tonight's lesson involved practical exercises like WAIT and OFF or FOUR ON THE FLOOR, which Dixie explained was the command for getting your dog to get off your company and keep four paws on the floor. As always, Dixie started by demonstrating each exercise with Chyna and Leia. We all struggled, but B.J. and Snowball struggled more than most.

"OFF! OFF! DOWN!" B.J. ordered, while Snowball danced around on her hind legs.

Dixie walked over. "First, you need to remember to give one command and only one. Let's try this." She gave Snowball the command to sit and stay, some of the first commands we learned. As soon as the Westie put her butt on the ground, Dixie rewarded her with a treat from the pouch she wore around her waist. Dixie turned to B.J. "Now, come toward us, but if she starts to get up, then I want you to walk away." B.J. walked toward Snowball, who immediately hopped up and started to jump. B.J. turned her back and walked away. Again, Dixie gave the command to sit and stay and B.J. walked toward her. Each time Snowball got up, B.J. walked away. It only took three times. By the fourth time, B.J. was able to stand in front of her dog and Snowball remained sitting.

"That was awesome. She gets the jackpot." Dixie reached in her pouch, pulled out a handful of treats, and gave them all to Snowball.

We learned early in training that when a dog worked hard to do something, "jackpot" meant a bigger than normal reward.

Dixie watched each of us practice and even used Madison and David as distractions.

"Make sure your dogs know they only get rewarded when they have all four paws on the floor." At the end of training, Dixie gave us our homework assignments.

Just as she announced the end of class, Beau entered carrying two large pizzas and pulling a cooler.

Around the corner was an office area with a table and chairs. Beau dropped the pizza boxes on the table. Dixie opened a file cabinet and pulled out paper plates, napkins, and cups.

"How are we going to eat with the dogs out?" Dr. Morgan asked as he struggled to keep his German shepherd, Max, from stealing the pizza.

Beau opened the cooler and pulled out a Ziploc bag, which immediately captured all of the dogs' attention. Inside were several large squares of a foul-smelling meat.

Monica Jill held her nose. "Eww, what is that stuff?"

Dixie smiled. "Liver jerky. I have it specially made for my dogs."

Beau handed each of the dogs one of the treats, which they took, then lay down and began chewing.

"Well, I'll be. What's in that stuff, doggie crack?" B.J. stared at Snowball as she nibbled on the square.

Dixie chuckled. "One hundred percent beef liver. I have a guy who owns a meat processing company. My dogs love it."

With the dogs distracted by liver jerky, the adults were able to sit at the table and eat in peace.

"That's pretty amazing. I've got to get me some of that liver crack." B.J. ate a slice of pizza.

"I'll give you his number." Dixie took a drink of her Diet Coke. "Now, what did everyone find out?"

Monica Jill raised her hand. "Let me go."

Everyone nodded agreement.

"I found out not only is Dallas and Keri Lynn's house for sale for an ungodly amount of money, but they have also listed the Pet Haven for sale."

Everyone seemed surprised.

"I thought they just opened," I said.

"Two years ago," B.J. added. "Well, I found out...oh, I'm sorry." She turned to Monica Jill. "Were you done?"

Monica Jill nodded.

"Well, I found out that someone"—she looked pointedly at Dr. Morgan—"someone has declared the accident suspicious." She smiled. "My insurance company is ecstatic. They just about pooped in their pants at the idea of paying out on her five-million-dollar life insurance policy."

"Five million dollars?" everyone echoed.

She nodded. "Yes, ma'am. I told you it was the largest policy I'd ever written. So I was ecstatic."

We turned to Dr. Morgan. He explained his concerns about the evidence of frostbite on Keri Lynn's toes and the other abnormalities in her autopsy. However, the biggest problem seemed to be the tissue samples he'd sent to have analyzed in Nashville. Apparently, they suggested Keri Lynn might have also been drugged.

We discussed the implications until there was nothing left to speculate about. Then Dixie and I told what we'd learned about Heather.

Madison and David had been eating quietly for the majority of the time.

When I finished, Madison said, "Well, today Mr. Simpson announced he was closing Pet Haven."

"Closing? Why?" I asked.

She shrugged. "He said Pet Haven had been Keri Lynn's dream and he just couldn't go on without her."

David looked at me. "He was very emotional."

"I guess that explains why Pet Haven is up for sale," Dixie said.

Monica Jill looked shocked, but then pulled out her phone and scrolled through several screens of messages. Eventually, she stopped and read. "That doesn't add up." She put her phone down. "My friend said he put Pet Haven up for sale over a week ago."

"Hmmm, so the entire time when he was saying Keri Lynn was alive, he was planning to sell it."

She nodded.

When the shock wore off, Beau cleared his throat. "Well, I talked to my friend who owns the Tesla dealership. He said the car was serviced three weeks ago and everything checked out just fine. However, those cars have a lot of software. They send information to the company all the time. So, if there was anything mechanically wrong, they would have known."

That reminded me of my conversation with Red. "But she wasn't driving the Tesla." I shared the fact that Keri Lynn had actually been driving Dallas's BMW.

"Well, that's odd." Madison stared. "I mean, she didn't like driving his car because it was a stick shift. Plus, with her being left-handed, she preferred the Tesla."

We talked for several more minutes but were left with more questions than answers. Eventually, we called it a night. We tossed our trash and practically had to drag our dogs away. In fact, I had to pick Aggie up to get her to leave. Even then, she clamped down on the liver jerky and left with it in her mouth.

David drove Madison home, and Aggie and I went home to think through all of the information we'd learned. Well, I did. Aggie continued to chomp on her foul-smelling treat on the back seat.

When we were home, I poured myself a glass of wine. Perhaps if I could relax, I could make everything make sense. I took a long, hot shower. I lacked Dixie's knowledge of dogs to get Aggie to voluntarily relinquish her treat. In fact, the only way I could get the liver away from Aggie was by tricking her with string cheese. There was nothing like the sound of a cellophane wrapper to distract a dog. She fell for the ruse, and I snatched the liver jerky.

Liver packed away, Aggie eventually stopped looking for it. Although I wasn't crazy about the look she gave me before she turned around so her back was to me and then lay down and went to sleep.

I tried to relax my mind. I breathed in and held the breath and then released it slowly. I thought back to the night of the murder. After a few moments, the tension in my neck relaxed the slightest bit, and I allowed myself to think about the storm. I thought about the kennels at Pet Haven, and before long, the image of the woman I believed to be Heather hosing down the kennels came into view. I saw her dressed in a raincoat and boots. She held the water hose.

I sat bolt upright in bed. "Oh. My. God." I tried to steady my breathing, but my heart raced. It was the only thing that fit. Like the tumblers in a lock, all of the pieces fit together, and I knew what had happened. There was one question I needed to answer.

I picked up my cell phone and called Dixie. "Can you give me Dr. Morgan's number?"

"Hello to you too."

"I'm sorry. I have a really important question I need to ask him."

I heard her rustling around. "It must be important." She fumbled with something, and then I heard a beep. "I just sent you his number."

"Great. Thanks." I hung up.

I quickly clicked on the contact information for Dr. Morgan she'd sent. It was only after the phone rang that I wondered if he was married. Thankfully, he answered the phone.

"When you examined the body from the accident, were there any metal plates or rods?"

He sucked in his breath. "How did you know? There was a metal plate in her foot and a rod. At some point, she must have had a really bad break that had required surgery and replacement of the bone with metal. How did—"

"Thanks." I didn't wait to hear the end of his question before I disconnected. I swiped until I found Red's number and pressed dial without thinking. It was only when I heard his groggy response that I looked at the time.

"I'm sorry to bother you, but I've figured it out."

"Figured what out?"

"I know how they did it. It wasn't Keri Lynn I saw murdered and Dallas wasn't the murderer. Keri Lynn and Justin murdered Heather, but Keri Lynn was behind it all. She convinced Justin to kill Heather."

"Why?"

"Insurance. She did it for the insurance money. Keri Lynn faked her death to get the insurance money. Heather looked like Keri Lynn. They were the same size and had the same hair color, and they looked a lot alike. Only Heather was right-handed and Keri Lynn was left-handed. That's why when she was hosing down the kennels, she had the hose in the wrong hand. She also wasn't wearing the expensive Rolex watch that Keri Lynn had." I smacked my forehead. "And the killer wasn't wearing Dallas's expensive watch either. How did I miss that?" I also explained about the plate in her foot that Heather told me about and that Dr. Morgan confirmed the body in the car crash had had.

I could tell Red was awake now, and if the rustling and breathlessness were an indication, he was quickly getting dressed.

"Why'd he do it?"

"Justin's naïve. I think she manipulated him…somehow she convinced him to help her. He probably thought he had to do it to get her to love him. Monica Jill said he'd do anything for Keri Lynn."

"Why'd she do it? If she was manipulating Justin, then why'd she care if her husband was having a fling with Heather?"

"She didn't kill Heather out of jealousy. She did it for the money, for the insurance money. Keri Lynn had a pattern of getting insurance money after a death. First her parents were killed in a car accident and she must have gotten the insurance money. Maybe that's what got her started. Anyway, she married her first husband, thinking he would make her a star, but he died." I paused.

"Are you saying she killed him?"

"I don't know. Stephanie said she was three hours away when he died. Although I'm guessing she had something to do with it. Maybe she tampered with the brakes or something. I don't know." I hopped up and paced around the bed. "He was a lot older than she was. Maybe she just thought he'd die naturally. I don't know, but she didn't get anything except a million-dollar insurance policy. His family wouldn't even make her films."

"A million dollars is a pretty good motive for murder."

"Five million is even better." I quickly explained about the five-million-dollar life insurance policy on Keri Lynn. "Keri Lynn has to be behind it. She was the one in the gas station video. She must have put Heather's body in that car and sent it over the cliff."

He rang off the phone with a promise to call me later.

I was too nervous to go back to bed, so I got up and dressed and made a cup of tea. Aggie must have forgiven me, because she got up and joined me in the kitchen.

Aggie and I were sitting on the sofa in the living room when David pulled in to the driveway.

"Don't tell me you were waiting up for me."

"Of course not. I'm waiting for Red." I took a sip of tea. I told him about Dallas and Keri Lynn's plans.

He made more tea, and we sat together and waited. It was very early before I got a text from Red. They had arrested Keri Lynn and Justin as they were boarding a plane for Greece. He promised to fill me in later.

"I can't believe you figured all of this out." David looked at me with awe and respect in his eyes. "You're like Sherlock Holmes or—"

"I prefer Agatha Christie." I scratched Aggie's head while she slept on my lap.

Red arrived at seven, and I could tell by the bags under his eyes and his wrinkled clothes, he had yet to go back to bed.

"I figured you'd want to know the details before you went to work." He yawned.

"Coffee?" I offered.

He shook his head. "It'll just keep me awake, and I'm planning to sleep for at least eight hours."

David joined us and we sat at the dining room table.

"You were right…about everything. Keri Lynn planned the entire thing. She encouraged her husband to start an affair with Heather." He shook his head. "One night when Heather was working late, she took her rain jacket. So, Heather was forced to wear hers."

"So she planned that someone would see it?"

He nodded. "She thought it likely. She made sure the footage was destroyed."

I frowned. "But that means..." I stared at Red, who nodded.

David was still confused. He looked from Red to me. "What? What does it mean?"

I shook my head. "It means she was setting up Dallas. If someone, like me, saw the tape and if the entire scheme fell apart, then Dallas would be blamed for the murder."

Red nodded. "She admitted as much. In fact, she laughed about it. Dallas would go to jail and she would just disappear." He rubbed the back of his neck. "So she stole Heather's identity and hightailed it to the mountains of Georgia."

I shook my head. "I should have remembered sooner that she didn't have any family. That whole family emergency thing was ridiculous."

He reached across and squeezed my hand. "She fooled a lot of people, including her husband. Dallas knew she was in Georgia, that's why he wasn't upset at first. He didn't get upset until I told him Keri Lynn was dead. He really thought she was alive."

"Did he know about Heather?"

Red shrugged. "Keri Lynn says he did. He says he didn't. He's blaming everything on Keri Lynn and Justin, which may be the truth, but that's up to the lawyers to work out." He squeezed my hand. "Stop beating yourself up. You figured it out in the end. In fact, if it hadn't been for you, she would have gotten away. They were boarding the plane when we caught them."

"So Keri Lynn planned this entire thing to get the five-million-dollar life insurance policy?" David asked.

Red nodded. "In fact, the real kicker is she changed the beneficiary on her policy just a couple of weeks ago."

"Who was her beneficiary?" David asked.

Red looked at me. "Wanna guess?"

"Heather?"

He nodded. "Bingo. She planned to start over as Heather and collect the insurance policy."

"But what about Dallas?" David asked.

"My guess is if he wasn't convicted for his wife's murder, then he would have met with an untimely accident."

"The poor sap," David said.

We asked a few other questions, but Red was so tired I decided to take pity on him and save my questions for later.

He declined my offer to take a nap. When Aggie and I walked him to his car, that was when I realized he wasn't alone.

A large dog sat on the front seat of the car.

I immediately looked for Aggie, who was completely unconcerned. In fact, her tail wagged, and she got in her play bow stance: butt in the air, shoulders down. I looked from Aggie to Red. "Who is that?"

"Heather's dog, Steve Austin. I was planning to take him to animal control. At the kennel, he seemed completely out of control. However, for some reason, he seems to have mellowed a lot."

I stared at the dog, then looked at Red and smiled.

"What?"

"Nothing, but I think Steve Austin just picked his new owner."

He looked confused. "Oh no. I don't think so. That dog is vicious. He most likely will need to be put down."

I was nervous, but something in my gut told me I was right. I walked over to the car and opened the door. Out jumped the pit bull/Labrador mix. He was a big dog, but I trusted my gut and I trusted Aggie's instincts. I tried not to notice Red's hand slide to his inside jacket and grip the butt of his revolver. We watched as Steve walked slowly toward Aggie. He sniffed her butt and then surprised us by giving a play bow. Front legs out in front of him, chest low to the ground, and butt in the air, he lay on the grass, tail wagging.

After a few moments, the two launched into a rousing game of chase in which the larger dog was no match for Aggie's speed. Several times he barely missed flying into the side of the car or a tree when she made a sharp turn at the last minute. However, the two dogs played until their tongues hung from their mouths and they lay on the grass, panting.

David had been watching from inside and came outside with a large bowl of water, which both dogs lapped up eagerly.

"Everyone said that dog was vicious." Red seemed confused.

"Maybe he was at Pet Haven. That's where his owner was murdered." I smiled. "However, I know Heather loved him, and I suspect he missed her a lot." I looked up at the scar on the side of Red's face. He and Steve Austin had both been through a lot. Like Aggie and I had searched for, and found our happy place, I hoped Red and this poor animal could both find theirs. With any luck, there'd be room for a widow and a pushy poodle when they did.

Printed in the United States
by Baker & Taylor Publisher Services